An Auspicious Beginning

Archana Prasanna

Dedicated to my grandmother, as she was the first artist I ever knew.

Contents

Preface

TO THE READER-

Before you begin, I would like to recognize the motivation behind the contents of this novella. The idea for this story emanated from my interest in the traditions of Indian classical music and the rich history of court musicians. The direction of the manuscript soon moved into the telling of a journey of following one's passion and reason for doing so. Furthermore, I have pondered the notion of destiny. I leave it to you, as the reader, to reach your own conclusion as to whether our purpose has already been determined by circumstances or must it be created by our own free will.

I have concluded, at our core, as human beings, we all have a desire to be seen, heard, and acknowledged, in some form or another. Our actions and motivations are all driven by this fact, perhaps.

This story is also a homage to teachers, of all kinds, be it from people or experiences, and the lessons we carry through the stages of life.

I hope you read this with an open heart and mind as I have attempted my very best to convey these musings.

-Archana Prasanna

Acknowledgement

First and foremost, I would like to express my gratitude to my parents, S. Prasanna and Kala Prasanna, for the love and encouragement they have showered me.

Furthermore, I thank my cousin Radhika Rangachar for lifting me up and supporting me with my writing.

For Chip, who is always by my side.

For my late uncle, S. Rangachar, who always encouraged my creativity and made me feel worthy.

And finally, for my late grandmother, Sarojawali Yoganath, for being the inspiration for my protagonist, as many of her nuances has been portrayed by this character.

1

INSIDE THE WOODEN BOX

Age had taken its toll on Leelavathi. Even with her glasses, she could not see very well these days. Fortunately the cataract clouding her right eye was not as severe as the one on the left, so it was still possible to carry out the stitching that occasionally needed to be performed on her old clothes. With winter approaching, it would soon get cold. There were new holes in a couple of sweaters that needed to be patched up.

Leelavathi sat by the window of her room and did the needlework as well as her old fingers allowed. Adjusting the frameless round glasses on the bridge of her nose, bringing the sweater nearer to the sunlight, she drove the needle in and pulled it up slowly. It had been nearly half an hour since she had applied herself to the job, but she had only managed to mend a couple tears. Leelavathi sighed. There had been a time when the same fingers had so much vitality in them that she could move them really fast. Any kind of stitch, however difficult it might have been was sewn with ease. But that was another time. Another era. That was another Leelavathi.

She had been a strong woman back then and an attractive one too, with smooth ebony skin and a sharp face with bright, clear eyes. When let loose, her thick jet-black hair would reach down to her waist. Nothing of that remained today. Time had taken away much of what she'd possessed. Her frame had shriveled, wrinkles had appeared on her skin, and her prized hair had thinned and greyed. Her fingers were bent and her once neatly trimmed nails had thickened and lost their shape. Now, everything she did with her withered, arthritic hands was a struggle.

Leelavathi adjusted her glasses once again and continued with the next stitch, immensely focused. It was not an easy thing to do. There were times when, with a sudden shift of the light outside or a gust of wind blowing into the room, her heart was overwhelmed, and without warning, sounds and memories of the past emerged in her restless mind. It was then that Leelavathi's old fingers would tremble and her eyes would become moist. It was in those moments that Leelavathi wondered if she could lock her emotions up for good as she had locked up her most treasured possession inside the darkness of the box, where it had been silent for so many years. But the mind is no wooden box; nor is the heart. They flood, and when they do, you can't just throw a lid on them.

Sewing helped Leelavathi remain rooted in the present. To keep herself occupied, she sewed whenever she could, not only her own clothes but also those of her great-grandson Rishab. Every afternoon at about this time, with the striking of the bell in the clock in her room announcing 3:00 p.m., Leelavathi eagerly awaited the boy's arrival. This ten-year-old boy never failed to bring cheer to her heart when he stepped into her room.

His parents were good people. They had been kind enough to take her in when they found out she could no longer manage her own affairs in her house. It had only been a few weeks since Leelavathi had come to live with them. Komal and Aryan had done everything possible to make her life comfortable. They had emptied a room, previously used as a storage space, for her. It was not a large room, indeed rather small compared to the one she had for herself in her own house, but big enough for an old woman like her. The one window opening to the street below brought in enough sunshine to keep it warm and bright.

But the sunshine Leelavathi truly craved was the young one, and if Rishab was late in coming home, held up by his teacher for his studies, Leelavathi could not help but think: *Isn't there a limit this boy can take into his little head?* But she was careful to keep her thoughts to herself. *This is not my own house,* she reminded herself again and again.

Leelavathi had reached the end of her thread and needed a new length. But there was no way she could manage threading a needle, no matter how hard she tried. She would have to wait for Rishab, who always managed to complete the task on a single try. He always took great pride in it, and Leelavathi acknowledged the feat, nodding and smiling. Everything the boy did or said brought pleasure to her.

Leelavathi put the needle and thread in the sewing box and folded the sweater she kept on the corner of her bed. Feeling a mild pang of hunger, she decided to eat a little more of the rice that Komal had brought. She went to a corner of the room where the bowl was placed on a low stool. Spreading an asana on the ground, she folded her legs and sat, took a little food and put it into her mouth. Leelavathi felt heat spread on her tongue. *The girl puts too much spice into everything she cooks,* she thought. So much that sometimes Leelavathi's stomach burned, too. She reached for the earthen pitcher, poured some water in the glass, and washed down her meal.

Leelavathi decided to take a nap on her bed to give her back some rest. It was a large bed occupying nearly half of the room. It had always been hers, one of the few large items that had moved with her into this new house. There was no other furniture in the room except for a rickety wooden table, a chair that stood by the window, and the low stool. Leelavathi kept her clothes in an iron trunk beside the bed. The few other items she needed she kept on the shelves carved out of one of the walls. The rest of her belongings still remained packed in boxes. Komal had shoved them under the bed so that the room remained uncluttered.

Leelavathi closed her eyes. In the few days she had been here, every time she woke up from deep slumber at night, she mistook the room for the one she had left for good. It took the mind some time to adjust in the semi-darkness of the dim lantern light, and there had been times when she'd risen from bed and walked in the wrong direction, only to collide with the wall. Coming back to her senses, realizing her present condition, an immense feeling of being uprooted often overwhelmed Leelavathi. Sometimes she shed tears sitting on her old bed, or she stood by the open window watching the empty street lit up by the gas lanterns. The mind took some time to console itself.

There were times when she had a great urge to lay her hand on the strings that had once been her life, to refill her soul with the sweet reverberations of her youth. But Leelavathi shelved the urges every time, as she had been doing for the past so many years of her life.

A commotion outside the open window made Leelavathi rise from her somnolence. She peeked out to see a horse-driven carriage that had gotten stuck between two bullock carts on the narrow street. The carriage driver was hurling abuse upon the drivers of the carts, who were trying their best to persuade their oxen to untangle the mess. One of the agitated bullocks swished its tail and nearly hit the face of the well-dressed gentleman poking his head out of the carriage window. The gentleman forgot the manners that accompanied his neat dress and elegant turban and hurled a curse. The bullocks began running so fast that both the animals and the cart fell into a roadside ditch. The bystanders watching the scene raised a commotion and ran after it. The horse carriage galloped away.

Leelavathi heard Rishab's laughter. The boy had slipped silently into her room and stood by her side, greatly amused by the scene unfolding below him. Now Leelavathi began to enjoy the scene too, and the two of them stood by the window as the bullocks and the cart was pulled out of the ditch. As the crowd finished the job and cheered, Rishab cheered too. He was a healthy boy with a head full of curly hair. His eyes were big and curious, radiating intelligence, and you could tell from his voice he was about to leave boyhood. He wore a full-sleeved round neck vest and a loose khaki-colored pantaloon that came down to his knees and was tied at the waist by one of her mother's ribbons. Leelavathi smiled at the boy as she ruffled his unruly hair.

"So, what did you learn today?"

Rishab beamed. "We started on a new novel. Do you know how to read this?" he asked, showing Leelavathi his textbook.

Leelavathi shook her head. How would she know? She didn't know how to read English except for a few words. When she was a child, very few people knew or learned English. British rule in the state of Mysore and the rest of the country was at its infancy then; only those who had to interact with the new rulers learned the language. Farsi, the language of the sultans, was still the language used for official purposes; Kannada was the language of the masses. Parents who had the means began sending their kids to schools run by missionaries where English was the main language of instruction. Rishab's father, Aryan, was an established lawyer in the civil court, and he had to conduct much of his job in the language of the rulers.

Good for those who move with the times, Leelavathi thought. *They find happiness. Those who can't and continue to hold on to the old and redundant, they suffer.*

"Now tell me, what is this?" Leelavathi pointed to the round thing the boy held in his hand.

"This is a cricket ball. I know you know that," Rishab said, rolling his eyes. "Let's play!"

Rishab thrust the ball into his great-grandmother's hand and moved back to the opposite wall. "Now throw it to me."

Leelavathi threw it as well as her feeble hand allowed her. The ball bounced weakly and went sideways, a long way from where the boy stood.

"Not like that! Throw it properly, in my direction!" Rishab picked up the ball, handed it to her, and went back to the wall again. "In my direction," he gestured.

Leelavathi tried as hard as she could. This time the ball headed for Rishab but hit a wall, ricocheted, and disappeared under the bed. Before Leelavathi could restrain him, Rishab went down on his knees and slipped under the bed frame.

"Be careful, don't hit your head," she called.

She could hear him in the darkness under the bed. What was he doing under there? What was taking him so long?

"Didn't you find it? Come out now. I will tell the maid to bring it out when she comes for cleaning."

The ball came bouncing out from under the bed. She waited for the boy to come out. But he did not.

"Come out now. What are you doing there?"

Finally she heard his voice muffled by the bed. "Coming," he called.

Leelavathi heard the sound of something being dragged. What was the boy up to? Moments later Rishab's legs appeared, followed by his torso. But his head was still hidden. By now Leelavathi understood that the boy had found something and was pulling it out with him. Finally he was out, and Leelavathi saw a piece of herself she had locked up years ago. Rishab stood up. The tip of his nose was blackened, and so were his elbows and knees. His eyes were filled with joy at his discovery.

"What is it? What's inside?" he asked eagerly.

On the floor was a fine box that emanated a strong scent of sandalwood, rectangular in shape and rather big, as big as him. But it was locked. An iron lock hung from a metal hinge on the lid.

Leelavathi stood, eyeing the box at her feet. When she had locked it for the last time so many years ago, she had vowed she would never unlock it again. But how could a promise an old woman made to herself stand up to the ardent pleas of a child she dearly loved? She hesitated.

"Where's the key?" he asked.

Reluctantly she showed him the key, in a pouch where she had stored it with some other valuables. As she held it in her hand, she suddenly couldn't resist putting it into the lock one more time. She opened the lid slowly as Rishab watched with excitement. What he saw inside left him agape.

"What is it?" He seemed stunned.

"It's a veena," said Leelavathi, smiling. "One plays music with it."

Her veena had remained as it was when she'd last put it inside the box, as immaculate as it had always been, though a little dusty. Time had not been able to harm it. Leelavathi found it difficult to contain the emotion wafting up in her chest. With moistened eyes she lifted the veena from the box. It felt very heavy in her feeble hands, but a new vigor came upon her as it always did when she laid her hands on the instrument. She held it for a while like a mother would hold her child, then placed it on the floor with great care, as if she would be hurting it if she were not attentive enough. The veena rested upon its two resonators.

Rishab brimmed with curiosity. He looked as if he had never seen anything so magnificent. The bigger resonator was made of wood with a flat surface from which emerged a neck that tapered and then curved downward, turning itself into a face of a dragon, which stared at the smaller resonator below that seemed to be made of gold. The many metal frets fixed on top of the neck, the strings passing over its entire length, the delicate ivory carvings running along the edges—every element of the instrument held the boy captivated. And much to Leelavathi's delight, it evoked his memory too.

"We have a picture of goddess Saraswati in our puja altar. She carried a veena like this one," Rishab said.

"Indeed!" Leelavathi ruffled the boy's hair in admiration. "This is the veena the goddess plays. And that is why it is called the Saraswati veena."

"Can I touch it?"

"Yes, of course."

Rishab laid his hand on the veena. Grazed his fingers along its different parts. The metal aspects of the instrument seemed to have caught his imagination more than the wooden ones. He patted the brass surface of the smaller resonator, ran his fingers over the bell metal frets, brushed them over the strings. The sound he created made him beam. Leelavathi took hold of the boy's index finger and made him pluck a melody string while pressing her own fingers on the frets. The resultant effect made the boy gape.

"Music!"

"Well, almost. Let me tune the strings first." Leelavathi turned the pegs, one by one, and then made him pluck some more. Rishab was ecstatic at having been able to achieve the feat. Then he looked up in wonderment.

"You know how to play it, don't you?"

Leelavathi nodded, smiling secretively.

"Show me." Rishab took his finger away and moved aside, making space for Leelavathi.

Her fingers no longer had the strength and maneuverability they'd had decades ago when she had last played the instrument. Yet she could not say no. She would refuse others, but not this boy. Leelavathi told Rishab to close the door. She did not want others to hear and draw undue attention toward her. The boy did as he'd been told. Leelavathi then took the veena upon her lap, placing the small resonator on her left thigh and the bigger one on the ground to her right. Rishab sat down, cross-legged like her. Leelavathi's fingers trembled. She closed her eyes and touched the strings. She paused for a brief moment, then she began playing.

It was like magic. The old, feeble fingers that took an eternity to pull up a stitch were suddenly injected with life. Plucking the strings and pressing the frets as effortlessly as she always had, Leelavathi stirred up a melody so enthralling that even a child with no sense of music sat mesmerized, unable to think of anything else.

After playing for about ten minutes, more than she'd intended, and finding herself powerless to withdraw her fingers from the strings even if her mind told her to, Leelavathi finally stopped. She had difficulty seeing the boy. Tears welled up in her eyes.

Rishab looked at her in awe. "You're a musician?" he asked, stunned.

"Well," she said reluctantly. "I was." Rubbing her eyes dry, Leelavathi smiled.

"It seems as though you still are."

Leelavathi smiled again. A sigh came out of her chest. Yes, she was still a musician, but what was left of her music, and of her, was only a residue, the last light that lingered on the horizon long after the sun had set.

"How did you learn to play it? Who taught you?" the boy asked. Rishab began hurling questions at her.

"I'll tell you one day."

"No, please, tell me now! Please," he begged.

She looked at him and thought, *Perhaps this is the only chance I'll get to share my past.* After a long pause, she responded, "OK, but I have to start from the beginning."

The boy smiled and Leelavathi, sitting alongside her instrument, began to remember. Back to the days when the veena was the purpose of her life and how it sustained her. She had a story hidden away, until now, when it all came flooding back.

2

A REGAL HOME

My father, Pandit Srinivas Iyengar, was a tall man with broad shoulders. His eyes were deep; a well-maintained mustache with curled ends complemented his strong-willed face. Except inside the house, he always wore a black achkan over his dhoti. My mother, Kalavati, was tall too, and slim. Years of thankless toil under ungrateful in-laws had taken away some of her shine, but not all of it. Her eyes were dark and dreamy; a soft smile hung at the edge of her lips most of the time. I had two brothers. Murali, my twin, my rival in every way. He was slender with bright, mischievous eyes. Jatin, the eldest of the three of us, was a strapping youth of sixteen with a body like my father's. He, too, had a burgeoning mustache that he had begun to take care of, though it was much thinner than Father's and not curled at the ends.

It was the time before Indian men had begun wearing pantaloons and long before fancy carriages thronged city streets creating chaos. I was then a little girl of five, slender and carefree, wearing a sari half the size of mother's, my abundant hair tied neatly by her in two long braids. After leaving our ancestral village, packing ourselves and our meager belongings into two bullock carts, and traveling for three days and nights, we had finally arrived in the city of Mysore.

We rode alongside a long, high wall on the main arterial road of the city until finally our carts stopped in front of a massive gate. The sentries on guard inquired of us, then let us in. A guard on horseback led our carts to our destination. Inside the hooded carriage of the first cart, I sat snuggled between mother and Murali. My heart thumped with excitement; I found it impossible to believe what I was seeing. Surrounded by an engulfing garden full of flowers and manicured hedges, and fountains that shot trails of water high into the air, stood a colossal palace several stories high and spread over acres of land. It had arches and hundreds of windows, with a towering dome at the very center. In our long and arduous journey through so many towns and villages, I had seen many new things and marveled at them. But what I saw, in all its grandeur, was awe-inspiring.

"The Maharaja lives here?" I asked my mother to confirm what I already knew.

Mother nodded, smiling. Laying her soft hands on my shoulder, she said, "Yes. And from now on we are going to live here too."

I looked at Murali as he giggled in excitement. On the cart in front were my father and Jatin. Together we all had embarked upon a new chapter of our lives. What we'd left behind did not bother us. Years ago, my father had set out to find recognition for his music, leaving the rest of us in the village where, in a large joint family of many cousins, uncles, and aunts, we lived as shadows, always taunted and tormented as being outcasts. It was an unusual way of life to pursue art as a Brahmin, something the other villagers found eccentric and uncultured. Now, a musician in the royal court of Mysore, Father was taking us to a home that we could call our own.

The horseman led our carts along a periphery road to the rear portion of the palace. Through an arched gate, we entered into a conclave where eight stone buildings stood around a courtyard.

"That must be our quarter," Mother said, pointing to a house. Brimming with anticipation, we entered. We had three rooms now and they were much bigger, adorned with decorative carvings on the edges of the ceilings and around the frame of the doors and windows that had bamboo screens on them. The kitchen was extensive. And a veranda opened up to a blossoming garden.

Mother entered the house looking as astonished as I did. She was excited to have a home of her own. Wrapping the end of her sari around her waist, she paused for a moment, gathering the surroundings, before she began setting up her domain.

"Look! I can garden here!" she said as she pointed outside.

Father had brought in much of the furniture and many utensils earlier, so Mother did not have to begin from scratch. The rooms were allotted. Jatin and Murali were to share a room between them. Another room would be the practice area, where Father could play his veena. The room that remained was for Father, Mother, and me. I had always slept with Mother by my side and I would not let the privilege be taken away.

The next morning we all woke up early, still reeling from the excitement of the move. The sun had barely come up before Father decided to take us on a tour of the palace complex and city. We walked from one conclave to another through the arched corridors that separated them, moved along an array of courtyards, some big and some small, beholding excitedly the many buildings surrounding them—some made of stone and some made of wood, some more gorgeous than the others. On courtyards of residential blocks, I noticed children playing for the first time. It didn't occur to me that other families would be here too. A few boys were running after one another, and little girls huddled in corners. The non-residential parts of the palace complex buzzed with activity, with people milling around on foot, and sentries and officials on horseback. I was interested in everything I saw, but the place I was most eager to go was the section where the royals lived—the section of the palace with arched facades, domes, and towers, surrounded by the gardens with fountains, that I'd seen when we first arrived.

We came to the grand bazaar that sheltered an array of shops under one roof. Everything seemed to be for sale amid the crowds and noise. Mother told Father what she was missing from her household and he bought the items for her there. There was no need to carry them with us, Father said;

everything would be delivered. I did not have to wait for my bangles, though. With help from Mother, I had them on my wrists as soon as they were bought. We traveled past a parade ground for soldiers, a stable full of horses and another of elephants, and a cage as big as a building, full of birds. There were several temples inside the palace walls. Mother offered prayers at several of them. One was on top of a hill. As I walked up and down the steps, my legs began hurting. Then finally, traveling up a steep path, we came to the front of the palace. Standing in the massive courtyard, we saw it in its true glory.

"There it its," Father said, almost looking intimidated.

Yesterday we'd entered by a side gate so we could get only a lateral view from a distance. Now, standing in front, was an entirely different experience.

"This is where he lives. The Maharaja," Father continued.

This part of the palace was particularly grand, with towers on the flanks topped by pink domes. In the middle stood a golden tower, with a golden dome that rose above the city. On the front was a façade, with many beautifully decorated arches standing on columns that were no less elegantly ornamented. Beyond the façade was a portico of polished marble, and beyond the portico, more columns and arches dividing the interior into two tiers, leading to a space that could not be seen from our vantage point.

Father pointed in that direction and said, "There is the durbar hall. The Maharaja holds his court in the durbar in the mornings. And in some evenings he entertains his friends and guests with music and dance."

"Is that where you play your music?" Jatin asked.

Father nodded yes.

"Can't we enter?" I asked, desperately wanting to see where Father would perform.

He shook his head, smiling. "Not today. It requires special permission from the Maharaja's office for people to enter the durbar. Even still, it is only for dignitaries."

"But you are a dignitary. You can visit the durbar every day," Jatin said.

Father laughed. "I am not a dignitary. I am only a servant of the Maharaja. And servants are not dignitaries. We can enter only to perform our art, and even still, by a different entrance, not this one."

I was not at all pleased to learn of my father's status and felt disappointed when he told us that the entire front portion of the palace above and around the durbar hall was comprised of royal quarters that we could not enter. But I was easily distracted as a carrier elephant passed us. We had seen many such carrier elephants on our journey through the city. The howdah box of this one was surely more gorgeously decorated, but that did not catch our attention. Who was the man seated inside it?

"Must be the Maharaja!" I nearly screamed.

Father shook his head and laughed. "No, he is not the Maharaja. He is a firangi."

Stunned, we stood looking at the man as he descended from the howdah, helped by some of the palace staff. This was the first time we had seen a firangi.

"Must be an important official," said Father. "They come to visit the Maharaja often these days. Let's head home now. It's getting late."

On that summer afternoon, with a gentle breeze blowing and puffs of white clouds skimming freely across a clear blue sky, we finally felt settled. After having the first dinner in our new home that Mother cooked in a kitchen that was exclusively hers, we sat on the veranda and talked late into the night. Father began re-telling us about the places he had been and the many experiences he'd had before finally coming to Mysore. He played concerts in the deserts of Rajasthan and the mountains of the Himalayas.

"One time, I performed for a yogi, close to Nepal. In the north. It is another type of richness there."

As Father told his stories, my eyes began to feel heavy. Both the full moon that had risen in the sky and the burning torches fixed on the palace walls lit up the entire area. From our balcony we could see that the city beyond the palace walls had fallen asleep; scattered across the dark vistas, sleepless lights flickered on. A gong sounded in the distance announcing the eleventh hour of the night. When it fell silent, the world fell silent, too, except for the occasional sound of horses trotting by or sentries on round. Father told us again about his musical journey. He enjoyed reminiscing on how he'd first perfected his skill, learning from his own father. It was only later that he traveled the country, giving performances in houses of rich patrons and courts of royalty before being admitted in the royal court of Mysore as a musician. He had finally reached the pinnacle for a musician.

Seeing Jatin no longer with us, I rose from Mother's lap and went inside to look for him. I found him in the drawing room. In the light of an oil lamp, he sat before father's veena, inspecting it. His own veena, which he had brought along with him, lay at his side. In spite of receiving the same taunts and sarcasm from other family members that Father had been subjected to, Jatin had followed in Father's footsteps, and had gotten himself trained by Father. I laid my hand on Jatin's shoulder. He turned to me and smiled.

"This is such a high-quality veena. Mine is nothing compared to it," he said.

I looked at the two instruments. The one that belonged to Father definitely looked more elaborate compared to the other, but beyond that I did not see any difference. I knew nothing about the instrument and the music created on it back then; I only enjoyed hearing it when Jatin had played for us back in the village. Little did I know in that first night of our arrival what the future had in store for me.

3

TWINS

The fondest and earliest memories of living in the palace were when I would awaken before dawn to hear Father playing his melodies. I could see him through the crack in the half-opened door, sitting upright and cross-legged on the ground, embracing his instrument, stirring up an unworldly melody. I wasn't allowed inside his scared room; the room where spent countless hours immersed in practice. I could however hear the music, and at that time, that was all that mattered. It is his improvised music that is forever etched in my ears. Mother's long hair had been loosened and waved in the breeze coming through the house as she also listened intently. With every notation Father rendered, she tapped her feet with such grace. The nupurs tied to her ankles resonated in perfect harmony with the reverberations of Father's magical rendering of the strings. It was as if she was accompanying him with rhythm. Under the mellow light of the early morning moon, they complemented each other in unison. I watched as if I were in the middle of a dream that I did not wish to end, but alas, I would fall back to sleep with a feeling of peace and contentment.

Our daily lives soon settled into a pattern. Father and Jatin would awaken before the sun had a chance to rise and bathe in cold water no matter the season. They would then offer prayers before their practice would begin. Once they did, they began with the basic scales, then more intricate note patterns, then slow melodies, and finally a composition. Father often looked like he was in a trance, as if he were not among us anymore. Oftentimes other court musicians would come to the house to play alongside Father. They would all bring their respective instruments and perform together. Everyone would be immersed entirely in the music, oblivious to everything around them, disturbed not even by the occasional clamor created by myself and Murali.

Murali and I were only two minutes apart. We were born on Akshaya Tritiya, when the sun and the moon align in such a way making it the brightest day of the entire year. Jatin had been born with a defect in his hearing, making him partially deaf. This limited his musical ability, no matter how hard he tried. Thus, Father was relieved when Murali was born, hoping he could one day carry on his legacy. When Murali took his first breath, Father carried him away from Mother and immediately whispered a prayer in his ear. He prayed that he would be the greatest musician India had ever seen. He then began singing musical notes to Murali, even before he finished his first cry. I never received any prayers as I took my first breath. However, I knew I was also born on that auspicious day. Perhaps my prayers were written in the stars for me.

Murali was at the age where he was ready to be initiated into the mysteries of the veena. An entire day was allocated to his initiation. Mother prepared foods and sweets and brought home a variety of flowers. Jatin carefully dusted and tuned the brand-new veena that had been bought for my brother.

"One day, I'll also play for the Maharaja. Will you come to watch me?" Murali asked me.

"No, never." I coldly replied. Envy had consumed me.

"You think the Maharaja will adorn me with jewels and gold? When I take the stage I'll need them."

"You'll never be like Father," I sneered.

"Leela!" Mother scolded.

"I will, too. He'll teach me everything."

It was under my father's tutelage Murali was to begin his apprenticeship. Father began grooming him with particular attention from that day forth. He was invited to the practice room to train alongside Jatin.

Murali however, struggled with the music. He cried often and that made Father only yell some more.

"I don't understand what you're playing," he often complained.

"Use your ears, boy!" Father would shout. "Again! Play the scale again!"

I found some amusement in hearing Murali get told off. I secretly hoped Father would ask me to replace him. The novelty of eavesdropping on the commotion that often occurred during his lessons quickly wore off. I sought out other ways to entertain myself as I no longer had Murali to play with. I began using my voice to practice the notes that were being taught. Mother often overheard me singing the scales and encouraged me in the hope that it would distract me from the growing resentment boiling inside of me. With the sound of Father's or Jatin's music coming into the kitchen, she would sometimes break into a dancing spell timed to the muffled sound of the veena strings to entertain and cheer me up. These were our private moments in which we giggled and tried to forget the restrictions put on us. I tried my best to imitate her, gyrating the way she did, taking the same postures, moving my hips, arms, and legs, rotating the hands, elongating and curling the fingers.

***

An entire year had passed since Murali had been initiated into the veena. His progress however, seemed to be going backwards. As such, arguments between Father and Mother were becoming frequent.

"He doesn't have it. He doesn't have music in him." Father seemed worried.

"He just started. Give him a chance."

"Who is going to carry on this legacy?"

"Your legacy!? There are other things to worry about now."

"I'm worried about this."

"Then teach Leela. You have another child that is eager for your attention."

Mother said sternly.

"Leela! Don't be silly. She's a girl, she has no place on stage."

"I've heard her sing, she listens to your lessons. Teach her, she has the talent," Mother pleaded.

"That's enough! Fetch Murali for me, he needs to practice."

One evening while Mother and I sat on the bed, she braided my hair as she did every day, Mother noticed me glancing at the veenas that were resting in the adjoining room. "Leela, maybe, just maybe, one day he will teach you too," she whispered.

I paused, not knowing how to respond as the thought had never occurred to me.

"Maybe." I whispered, under muffled breath. It was her words that planted a seed, that perhaps I could enter the practice room one day as a student. I was never invited into to practice, so perhaps I would have to take it upon myself.

4

THREE TESTS

One evening, at the request of my mother, my brothers left the house to gather some items from the market.

"Mangos, bring the ripe ones." she instructed. "Don't eat eat them all on your walk home!" she yelled as the boys were out the door. "Leela, I need to water the flowers, I'll be just outside."

Father had left for the durbar and Mother was busy in her garden. The house was eerily quiet. I quickly realized that I was all alone, for once. This was the first time I was on my own and an idea that I had been scheming for this very moment could finally happen. I had a chance to play the instrument that I wanted to get my hands on. *This was my chance,* I thought to myself. I snuck into the practice room as quietly as I could and stood by the door, admiring the polished instruments that lay on the floor. My stomach churned with anxiety and my fingers itched to touch them. I slowly made my way towards Murali's veena and sat by it. At first, I merely pretended to strike the strings and imagined myself giving a concert to the Maharaja himself. I didn't touch anything, scared the noise would alert mother. But I couldn't resist. Eventually, I began plucking one string. The vibration shook my tiny body. I then plucked another string. And then two together, making the sounds resonate. And then three strings. Then each individually, note by note. At first, I aimlessly strummed, not knowing what I was doing. Then I remembered, *I knew father's lessons.* I tried to remember the scales I had overheard Father teach and I replicated that on the veena. Then, a composition Father had taught Jatin was etched in my head. I so desperately wanted to play it that I began my attempt to reproduce what I had heard. Sweat poured down my forehead as the veena was too heavy for me and my arms were too short. I struggled to find the correct note on the fret and grew frustrated, but eventually one note sounded correct. Then two. Then slowly, the composition came together. A melody. I was playing music. I was immersed in the sound and overcome with joy. I stayed there, playing, forgetting everything around me, in a trace like state.

"What are you doing?" Father yelled.

Startled, I didn't know what had just happened. I took a minute to come to my senses and realize what I had been doing. I didn't know what to say or how to respond.

"You shouldn't be playing on this! Get out!"

My face began to feel warm and wet. I felt tears running down my blushed cheeks. Ashamed, I jolted up and decided to run and left the house. I just kept running. I became acutely aware of how sore my fingers had become from pressing down on the strings. That pain made me cry even more. I kept going, outside the palace gates, even as it began to rain. The monsoon had arrived and the pellets of water hammered my tiny body. But I kept running—from what, I didn't know.

✳✳✳

The time I spent out in the rain made me bedridden with a high fever. Even worse, not being able to play music made me sad within. I took out my anger and jealousy on Murali.

"I brought you some jasmine flowers," he said as he entered my room.

"Go away!" I shouted.

The few moments I had with the instrument had brought out an element in me that I had not been aware of before. It was the ability to lose myself, in a way that was so intimate yet so unrestricted. And so joyful. Unable to do that anymore, I became melancholic just as the monsoon brought on the cool weather. Trying to maintain a composed face, I began looking for solitude from the birds I watched through the window. In the quietness of the afternoons when the palace complex fell into slumber, I slipped out of the room and went to the terrace. Roaming under a mellow sun, or sitting in an alcove letting the breeze caress me the way it wanted to, I let myself feel the deep pain I was trying to hide. I felt rejected by Father, but at the same time, I didn't know how to articulate that. I would find solace keeping my head on my mother's lap, sipping from her hand the broth she prepared for me and listening to the many stories she would tell me to make me give her a glimpse of a smile. It was then the burden weighing me down lifted momentarily. But that fleeting moment only lasted for so long.

I still felt empty like never before. My body was healing, but my spirit was not. I remained in the room for most of the month recovering, most of the time in bed staring at the wall.

Mother would often ask, "Leela, shall we go for a walk. I need to buy some fruits from the market. Come on, the fresh air will do you some good."

I refused.

"Look what you're doing to her. Just teach her!" Mother shouted.

"I can't! It's not her place!"

As they kept shouting, I covered my ears and began humming a song, trying to drown out the noise, until I fell asleep.

It was the next morning when I found Father sitting beside me.

"You want to learn? From me?" he asked.

"What?"

"You want to learn from me? Not until you can prove to me that you can handle my ways. Wake up, get ready and meet me outside."

With a throbbing head, I rose up and did what he said. Confused, nevertheless.

Outside was a large pile of jackfruits. "These fruits come from the tree the veena is made from. If you are to hold a veena, you need strength. Now carry each fruit to those carts over there. One by one."

I thought I misunderstood. It all seemed too absurd. "Carry the fruits?" I asked, massaging my head.

"Yes. This is what you and your mother asked of me, to teach you? This is your first lesson."

"But, there are hundreds of fruits here, how am I supposed to do this?" I asked with a tinge of fear in my voice. By the time I finished my sentence, Father had walked away. I waited, hoping he would come back, hoping he could help me or ask me to come back inside. He didn't. So I did as he asked. I began to carry each fruit, one by one, just as he requested. I carried them from dawn until dusk—my arms trembling, sweat pouring, feet aching, and my breathing seemingly too heavy for my chest. After toiling away for hours, I was finished. I did what was asked of me. I went home and fell on my bed, drained.

The next morning, Father woke me up again. "Get ready, meet me outside," he said. My aching body, reeling from the day before, once again did as he asked.

"Where are the jackfruits?" I asked, seemingly annoyed.

"Look here. With this pile of straw, make me a rug. One big enough for both of us to sit on."

"I don't know how to sew."

"You don't need a needle, just weave them together. Use your fingers. They need to be nimble."

I had seen the straw rug in the practice room and the design on it. I knew what to do. I just had to weave them together, overlapping each piece of straw. I worked again, from dawn to dusk. My fingers aching and cramping. But I finished, and I was proud.

The next morning, I woke up and bathed before Father had a chance to come and get me. But he didn't come and fetch me. I waited by the window, and waited some more.

"Where is Father?" I asked Mother while she cooked.

"He went to the durbar. He'll be back in the evening. Eat something, you look exhausted."

I was disappointed. Did I fail his lessons? I went about the day perplexed as to what I had done. Father never came home and it was already time to sleep. I snuggled next to Mother and shut my eyes. Her warmth comforted me and all the pent up anxiety of the day went away. At least for a minute.

"Wake up, it isn't time to sleep." Father's words startled me.

I was on the verge of sleep, rather groggy, but I managed to ask, "What do you mean? It's bedtime."

"Come with me."

"Mother!" I shouted, asking for her help.

"I can't help you now. This is what you wanted."

I walked with Father to the practice room.

"Sometimes, we have to practice when we are tired and sleepy. Some ragas we only play at night; you can't be asleep if you want to hear these ragas. Stay awake with me while I practice these evening melodies."

I understood what Father was doing. I stayed awake and was attentive to what he played. I had never heard these compositions before. He practiced until the rest of the family woke up.

"The sun has risen, let's rest now." He finally spoke.

I collapsed onto my bed soon afterward. On the brink of sleep, Father and Jatin were standing by the bed.

"This is for you," Jatin smiled as he presented a majestic veena to me. My very own. "From now on, you'll be practicing with us."

I looked at Father. He nodded. "We start tomorrow, early."

I finally fell asleep with a smile on my face.

***

The strict regime Father forced upon me began immediately. I would not want it any other way. Mother had to nudge me out of sleep the first few mornings and then carry me to the bathroom to pour cold water to drive the remaining sleep out. On the first day of my apprenticeship, she made me wear a new sari after bathing. We went to the drawing room. Father, Jatin, and Murali were already there. Mother told me to touch Father's feet and then Jatin's. Father blessed me, placing his hand over my head, muttering his blessings with his eyes closed. Then he tied the ganda on my wrist. It was a thread that the teacher tied to the disciple's wrist to mark the beginning of his musical journey. We sat before our veenas, I before mine. Closing his eyes, Father chanted an ode to the goddess. We repeated after him. Mother watched, sitting on the side, her eyes flooding. She had not been there when her sons had been initiated, but for her daughter she did not mind foregoing her cozy early morning sleep.

I was small. Father could have brought a smaller veena for me to suit my yet-to-develop fingers and arms, but he did not. It was difficult at first to keep a grasp on it; my fingers got sore, my body ached. To give me some relief, Mother massaged my hands and arms with coconut oil. In a few months' time, I was able to master the strings; my fingers were moving freely over the frets and I had learned the basics, but what I was producing was just sound, not music. The journey had just begun.

Father was ruthless. Jatin, an apprentice to Father but teacher to us, was just the same. The days Father did not go to the durbar we practiced all day long, making Mother angry. "Won't you give her a break?" she would complain in the initial days, always thinking about my well-being over everyone else. It did not take long to begin to fall in love with my veena and the music it produced. I began to look forward to the arduous practice sessions.

The ability to produce the essence of each kriti, the sruti, the laya, the sahitya, and accurately playing the intricacies and nuances of each raga is what the vainika strives for, and it is not an easy endeavor. It takes years and years of practice and dedication to play even the smallest of kritis perfectly, and you can't do it if you are not deeply in love with your music. Every time I played a kriti, I learned new ways to add more nuances. The more I played, the more I understood what it took to attain perfection, and the road to perfection got longer and longer. And my love for music became deeper and deeper.

Then came a time when I was eating, sleeping, and breathing music. My veena and I became one. In the evenings with the setting sun coloring the horizon with hues of red, pink, and blue, I walked on the terrace listening to the chirping of birds returning to their nests, the ringing of distant temple bells and the different end-of-the-day sounds that rose from our courtyard. They all mingled with the music that reverberated inside me. My heart brimmed with such happiness. I felt perfectly content.

My love must have been manifesting itself during the practice sessions. Looking up from the frets, or after opening my eyes when I played with my eyes closed, I could see Father's and Jatin's admiring eyes upon me. Though they never said it and tried hard not to show it, I knew Father and Jatin appreciated my dedication more than that of my brother, and I, for my part, practiced with even more dedication in my endeavor to please them. Murali, on Father's advice, shifted to the mridangam much to his displeasure. He did much better with that instrument; soon he began accompanying us on the veena. Between her chores, Mother would come to the music room whenever she could. Sitting among us, she would listen to us playing and also to Father's talk about the various facets of carnatic and Hindustani music, the various aspects of the ragas, the life stories of various exponents, and their contribution to music. We learned about artists who enriched our music with their unparalleled contributions. As I matured with the instrument, I began envisioning a future that would go beyond the tiny room where all these lessons took place. I was preparing to make my mark as well.

5

THE PALACE DURBAR

As I matured over the years, I began to take greater notice of the events that took place outside my sheltered world of music. I began to take an interest in the conversations Father had with his colleagues and came to know that everything was not as exquisite and perfect as the palace presented itself. The firangis and their East India Company were wielding their power more than ever; the Maharaja now had to confront restrictions that were being imposed upon him on his style of running his court.

"They are deciding on protocols too," Father said one day. "On whom the Maharaja can meet and whom not. What he should be discussing and what not to discuss. There is a company representative always present during the discussions the Maharaja has with his ministers. They want to control everything."

"So the Maharaja is nothing more than a puppet," Jatin said.

"It seems so, yes," said Father.

Mother frequently averted any political conversation. "What does this have to do with any of us?" she remarked. "We are ordinary people leading our ordinary lives. Who controls what is not of our concern."

"Be thankful your husband is a musician," Father chortled in response. "The Maharaja is being forced to curtail much of his extravagance because of the tightening of his budget by the firangis. People are losing their jobs because of this imposed thrift. Hopefully music and art are something they will not encroach upon."

How wrong Father would be proven to be. Music, the vehicle that was supposed to build bridges between civilizations, smoothing over differences, turned out to be one of the worst sources of conflict between the Maharaja and the firangis. It was not a curtailment of the budget that created the rift, but something entirely different. And fatefully, it was my father who was at the center of it all.

It happened on the very day Father took us to the durbar to listen to his performance for the first time. It also turned out to be the last. Who knew then our stay in the palace was coming to an end?

We were all so thrilled when Father announced that he would be taking us to the durbar. I could not sleep all night. Mother, who remained calm in other situations, was excited too. She brought out our best clothes and fretted about our looks, forcing us to take hot baths with the most expensive soaps she had in her possession so that we sparkled and smelled like heavenly bodies. Providing limited attention to the men, she invested most of her energy on me and herself. By the time we were ready, the men, including Father, could not take their eyes off us.

"She has become a lady," Father said, looking at me, saving his compliments for his wife for later.

"She indeed is," Mother said smiling, fixing a bindi on my forehead. I blushed, feeling both shy and proud of my new status.

Welcomed by a palace official, we entered the durbar hall with thumping hearts. Whoever saw us came forward and greeted us. I felt so proud, witnessing firsthand the respect people had for my father. And no wonder I was flabbergasted with what I saw around me. If the palace exterior was magnificent, the interior was simply breathtaking. I knew from listening to Father what I would be seeing inside the durbar hall, but compared to what I actually saw, his account seemed rather mild. The space was enormous. Numerous tapering columns of bright blue and gold held upon themselves rows of golden arches and domed ceilings, arches intricately carved, the convex surfaces of the ceilings beautifully painted. Huge dazzling chandeliers hung from each, illuminating the length and breadth of the interior. Decorated vases and marble figurines stood at various corners; life-size paintings of the early kings and queens adorned the walls. The sparkling marble floor was so polished that I held Father's arm in fear of slipping.

At the end of the hall, against a backdrop of bright red curtains, stood a glorious golden throne. It was studded with gems, its triangular backrest decorated with a motif of a goddess and her worshippers. Marble steps from the side led to its spacious seat of brilliant pink. The person who would be occupying it had not yet arrived; a lone pillow of matching pink substituted for him for the moment.

In front of the throne, some distance from it, the musician colleagues of Father sat on the cushioned floor, tinkering with their instruments. Father's veena had already been placed there. Father sat before it. Flanking the space between the Maharaja's seat and that of the musicians were sitting arrangements for the audience on cushions laid on the floor. Many had already taken their seats. My brothers sat among the men; Mother and I were led to a section reserved for women. Our escort introduced us to the few women who were present, all wives of dignitaries of various status. They began chatting with Mother in a low voice, cuddling me and asking me questions that I answered half attentively. With the other half of my curious mind I looked around, eagerly awaiting the arrival of the Maharaja and wondering who would be sitting on the empty sofa that stood next to the Maharaja's throne. It was a very beautiful sofa meant for two people, with a frame of polished wood and turquoise upholstery, its seating height slightly lower than the Maharaja's throne. Being the only other above-the-ground seat besides the Maharaja's, it must be for very special people, I thought.

The wait finally came to an end. The Maharaja was announced and he appeared from a side door with his entourage, a golden umbrella held above his head by a royal servant. We stood up in his honor. I should have been awestruck at my first vision of the man whom I'd thought and dreamt of so much, and he looked very handsome indeed in his royal attire. But what wrenched my gaze away from him was the couple who walked in immediately after him, the young woman in particular, held by the arm by the man beside her.

They were both British officials. The man was middle-aged. Though very fair, he was not exactly good-looking, with big sideburns that came down to the middle of his cheeks; he was balding and more than half of his head shone in the light. He wore a suit and pantaloons and English shoes like those that many Indian people wear these days. Our Maharaja—with his bright smiling eyes and richly curled mustache, clad in a gorgeous silk chapkan fitted with an equally gorgeous belt from which hung his sword, his head adorned in the royal turban—was much handsomer than the Englishman. But the lady, she was breathtakingly beautiful, with blue eyes and bright red lips and a head full of golden curly hair. We had heard about people with golden and brown hair, but for the first time Mother and I saw one. What fascinated me the most was the dress she was wearing. I still remember it. She wore a beautiful mauve hat over her golden hair and it had flowers stuck on it. The tight jacket on her upper body was mauve too, and it had golden buttons. Underneath it, she wore a black skirt that fell to her knees beneath which her legs were completely bare except for the dazzling blue shoes that covered her feet. On her shoulder hung a yellow leather bag.

The Maharaja climbed the steps and sat on his throne cross-legged. On his signal we all sat, our feminine gaze not on our Maharaja or anything else, but upon the astonishing specimen of our tribe. She sat beside her partner, one leg on top of the other. An announcer read out the names of the dignitaries present at the occasion; the first names were of the English couple: Mr. and Mrs. Simpson. Mr. Simpson was the new highest representative of the East India Company in our part of the country.

After the announcements, Father began his recital. He started with a new composition he himself had composed. It was based on raga bhairavi. He did not take long to captivate the audience with his superlative rendering, studded with skillful ornamentations. The audience listened, mesmerized;

many nodded their heads in appreciation as the composition proceeded. Lost in his music, Father played with his eyes closed as he always did. I looked up and saw the Maharaja too, had his eyes closed. Resting his chin on his hand, he listened with deep contemplation, as lost as Father. My heart brimmed with pride. I looked at Mother and saw her moist eyes. Jatin and Murali listened attentively, looking at Father, their faces lit up with pride no less intense than mine.

Even though I had begun learning music and hence I should have immersed myself in Father's renderings as did the rest of the true listeners, I was still a curious girl with a wandering mind, and so my gaze traveled from Father to the Maharaja and others. Most of the time I found myself looking at Mrs. Simpson. She did not seem to be appreciating the music and neither did her husband. They seemed to be bored; Mrs. Simpson was somewhat restless, her eyes roving all around the hall. Once, her gaze met mine and I thought she smiled at me. Feeling shy, I looked away.

Father ended the first composition. There was a lot of applause from the audience, including Mr. and Mrs. Simpson. Once again I brimmed with pride. Father began his second composition. It was a Tyagaraja composition, based on raga kalyani.

As he played, my eyes went to Mrs. Simpson once again, and this time I saw her taking something out of her bag. Curiosity got the better of me. Forgetting everything else, I stared at her. Mrs. Simpson brought out a little box and, after opening it, looked inside. Then she brought from her bag what seemed like a small pencil and with it she rubbed her lips. I had no idea what she was doing.

But the Maharaja knew. I saw him looking at Mrs. Simpson from his throne, his face grim. He suddenly turned toward Father, raising his hand.

"Stop," he said, rather expressionless.

Father, startled, muted the strings with his hands. All eyes then went to the Maharaja, including those of the Simpsons. The uncomfortable silence made my heart beat fast. The Maharaja looked at Mrs. Simpson and said something I could not hear. Mrs. Simpson's white face turned blush red and so did Mr. Simpson's. The two sat stunned for a moment. Then Mr. Simpson rose and, catching his wife by the arm, pulled her up and dragged her out of the hall. Unmoved, the Maharaja saw them leave and then told Father to continue. Father started afresh. The concert continued as if nothing had happened.

But something did happen. And it was grave.

"Father, what happened in there?" I asked.

"The Simpsons, they disrespected the court. The Maharaja asked them to leave and return once she was done with her make-up. Don't worry, it won't happen next time." He smiled.

***

News of the incident at the durbar began to spread. First, among the palace officials and residents, and then beyond the palace walls. The fallout was catastrophic. The cultural aspects of the palace had so far remained immune to British influence, until now. The evening after the incident, Father went to the durbar as he usually did.

"No recital today, Pandit. Go home," a palace guard told him.

"I don't understand, what happened?"

"The Maharaja, he's…sick," the guard responded rather unconvincingly.

The court remained closed the evening after, and the next, and for the entire week. The same reason was cited: the Maharaja was unwell. But by then it had become known to everybody the true reason for the court's closure.

"He isn't sick. The firangis have something to do with this," Father whispered to his colleague as they both walked home. "It is happening. They are going to take over."

The English had come down heavily with their retribution. They had barred the Maharaja from organizing any sort of musical event, and so there could be no performances.

The impact was telling on Father and his musician colleagues. They would gather in our house and discuss worriedly what the future held in store for them. In spite of the prevailing uncertainty, Father would not waver from the strict practice regime he had set for himself and the rest of us. We continued with our lessons as usual, until he was requested to be back at the durbar.

"Pandit!" A neighbor came rushing into his practice room. "Something has happened."

"What's the matter?"

"The durbar. There is immense pressure from the English; the Maharaja has been asked to destroy all the musical instruments in the court. From now on, only Western music is to be played in the court."

It was rumored that the English wanted to introduce Indians to instruments like the piano and the violin. An orchestra from London was on its way to give the first performance of its kind. Father digested the news calmly and then sat with his veena for a long time. All his anxieties he washed away with the sound of his veena.

The evening of the very next day, the Maharaja called Father into his private chamber. He was told to come with his instrument.

"Play for me, one last time," the Maharaja requested, solemnly.

Sitting before the Maharaja and his queens, accompanied by a mridangam player, Father performed for a long time, playing one composition after another. That was Father's last performance before the royals and in the palace. After the recital, the Maharaja informed the duo about the designs of the firangis and his helplessness to do anything about it. The only concession he had been able to obtain from them was permission to retain his best musicians, on the condition that they train themselves to learn the Western style of music. The mridangam player conceded, agreeing to switch over to the drum, however difficult it might be to learn a new instrument in an entirely different style.

But my father refused point blank. He would not part with his veena come what may. The implication of his refusal was obvious. The Maharaja offered monetary assistance, which Father refused to accept. He said to the Maharaja, "You have given me so much already; all the recognition and respect a musician could hope for I have gotten from you. For that I will be indebted to you all my life. There is no need for anything more." The Maharaja hugged my father and wept, and told his queens to touch Father's feet.

6

COMING OF AGE

We left the palace. It was difficult for all of us, but most of all for me. Mother did her best to hide her tears. I could not stop my eyes from overflowing as we left the palace compound with our belongings, this time in a horse-driven cart rather than one hauled by bullocks. Father had rented a house in the outskirts of the city, a three-room apartment much smaller than our palace house, and we moved in there. It is not easy to adjust to your circumstances if you are being demoted in status, but we tried our best. In spite of the pain each of us suffered, we continued our music practice as assiduously as before.

We had some savings but they were limited. Father had to earn money to keep the family wheel turning. There were rich patrons whom he knew. Initially some of them invited him to their houses to perform. Accompanied by Jatin, he gave private recitals and was being paid for it. But it did not take long for those invitations to dry up. The palace was the center of cultural activities, and anything that happened inside the palace had repercussions outside. Afraid of the wrath of the English, even the most ardent admirers of Father's veena recitals were reluctant to patronize him beyond a point.

Father understood their dilemma. Not wanting to get them into trouble, he declined even the few invitations that came his way.

Mother tried her best to run the family with the meager resources. But it was getting more and more difficult by the day. Then one evening, after dinner, Father called us to the drawing room for a family meeting. He told us that he and Mother had decided to move to his ancestral village in the countryside. He had decided to buy some land there and start farming.

We did not say anything, but the surprise and shock must have been evident on our faces. So Father explained, "It is fertile land with a homestead. Not a lot of land, but not meager either. I have two healthy boys and I am not old yet. If we work hard, we will be able to feed ourselves well. It is much better to sustain yourself with your own means than to have to wait for others to give you work. As for music, it will always be with us. I have strived to make the world listen to my music all these years and have understood one very important thing: It is much more important for a musician to love his music than for the world to love it. I don't care anymore if the world listens to my music or not. From now on, I will be playing for myself and my dear ones only."

So we came to our new home in the country. It was on the edge of a small village, a night's bullock cart journey from Mysore city. Our homestead was surrounded by land on all sides. The house had five rooms, all bigger than the ones we'd had in the palace. There was greenery all around, and a gentle breeze always blew, rustling their leaves. Being on the periphery and surrounded by rows of big trees, our land was secluded from the rest of the village, which suited us fine. We did not want to segregate ourselves from other villagers, though; all we wanted was a little privacy.

It was difficult at first to adjust to the rural environment, having spent so many months in the city. We missed our palace and often mused about the time spent there, though not in front of Father. We all agreed that he had made a very good decision to come to the village. Our new life was heaven compared to the period of uncertainty we suffered following our departure from the palace.

Father and my brothers did not know much about farming, so it was difficult in the beginning. But our village neighbors were friendly and cooperative, and Father's music and palace background earned him and us a lot of respect from them. With their help and with the help of hired hands, we began tilling our land. Two pairs of bullocks were bought for this purpose. We also bought a couple of cows and hens. Mother, in her childhood, had some farm experience, so she was not entirely a novice. I definitely was, but still eager to learn. With guidance from our hired help, the two of us milked the cows and cared for the birds. It wasn't long before we were doing the farm work as efficiently and with as much dedication as the other farm women of the village.

Had there been no music in our lives, it would have been far more difficult. Music was the balm for the ache of our loss and also that of our bodies. Our day began with practice as it had in the city, but not nearly as much as we had done there. After two hours of practice and then eating breakfast, Father and my brothers went to the fields and I would accompany Mother to care for the animals. There was a lot of work to do. We would milk the cows together, collect cow dung, and lay the cakes on the floor where they would dry and later be used as fuel. Murali would chop the wood for us. We would collect eggs from the hens, feed the birds and animals, do all the cleaning, and water the flowers in our garden. We would go to the vegetable field to collect vegetables and then cook meals for lunch and supper. With the advent of the harvest season, we would go to the fields to assist the boys in cutting the paddy crop. Together we would do the stacking, threshing, and hauling jobs.

It was hard work for all of us. But with the love we had for each other, we gradually transformed ourselves from city people to perfect farmers, no longer rueing what we had left behind.

Father and Jatin, taking up the roles of our teachers, would give us lessons on various subjects in the evening. Then we would have supper. And then out on the verandah, sitting on its earthen floor, we would practice our veena with Murali on mridangam. Under the tutelage of our two teachers, interspersed with their alternately harsh and gentle admonishments and muted appreciations, we would hone our skills. With our hands and minds working to utmost capacity, we would learn the various nuances of our art, taking into our souls the essence. We would put our tired minds and bodies to rest after a few hours of practice. The sound of our instruments reverberating in our young ears, we would fall into deep, unobstructed sleep, intermingled with sweet dreams of our old palace days. And then, once again, we would wake up to a fresh, new day.

There were special nights when the moon washed our fields in a mystic silver light and the wind rustled the leaves of the trees in a soft murmur, calling to our mother. On such nights she would not remain indoors. We would go out in the open, set up our stage on the ground under a basil tree. Now I would be playing too. I would play as if in a trance, my heart brimming with joy. Our concerts would continue deep into the night, for we didn't want it to end. So happy we all were, seeing each other so happy and content.

If only we could have lived our lives as it was then, forever.

Seasons came and went; years passed one after the other. We were now full-fledged villagers, planting, growing, and harvesting our sustenance with hard work but softened by music, the food of our soul. Now I was truly a young woman, and an attractive one who caught the eyes of many village boys, making Mother worry for me like never before. I was nearing twenty. Rarely at that time would you come across an unmarried girl of that age. Father was not yet fully prepared to let go of his dear daughter. Though he no longer had the luxury of holding on to his principle of not condoning early marriage, he fell back on the only excuse that was now left to him: the eldest child should be married off first. However, Jatin hadn't agreed to a marriage just yet, and the pressure remained on me.

I won't say I had not been interested in marriage. Far from it. To be honest, I was eagerly looking forward to the day when Jatin married and the search for my groom would begin. But a feeling of reluctance crept up on me as the notion of marriage was turning into reality. I did not want to leave my family and go to a new home, yet again. But Mother seemingly brought up the subject again with new vigor, this time with much more urgency and a lot of petulance as well, raising her voice against Father, forcing him to hurry in his search for my groom. Though I was quite attractive, the fact that I was from a peculiar family and being a vainika in my own right—a vocation I had made clear I wouldn't disown after marriage—compelled many families not to proceed with the match. The other two conditions that we had set, that I should be the only wife and not to any over-aged man, didn't help the process either.

Alas, despite all the hurdles and to the surprise of many, a match was near finalized, with a man eight years older than I. He was the only son of his parents and a late arrival, conceived after years of praying to the gods and numerous visits to temples all over the land. They lived far away, in a small town in another district, scores of miles from our home. And they asked for dowry. Father was reluctant, but upon Mother's insistence he agreed to pay.

Within a few weeks, a wedding took place. On the eve of the event, my Mother pierced my nose with a thin piece wood she had sharpened with a knife. Mother adorned me with the few ornaments that Father had bought for her during his affluent palace days. I was dressed in a bright red silk sari that Father bought for me from Mysore. It was expensive. There was not much money left after the hefty dowry of cash that had to be paid, but my parents wouldn't compromise on their only daughter's attire. Nor on other wedding expenses, which included, among other things, feeding the entire village, as well as cartloads of guests who came from my in-law's village in spite of the distance.

My soon-to-be husband had been left out of the selection process, just as I was. His father, mother, and uncles had come to see me. So it was at the marriage ceremony that my husband and I saw each other for the first time. He turned out to be more or less as he had been described to me, a mild-mannered man with a pale complexion, but sober, gentle looks. Not exactly strong, but taller than I by a couple of inches. His face was narrow and the lips thin, over which he grew a rather gorgeous mustache. I was not exactly impressed but was not aghast either.

I felt as if I were being torn from my real body when they took me away. Our family façade of stoicism gave way. Mother wept madly, showering me with kisses. His legs barely moving, Father walked me to the palanquin, tears flowing from his eyes. Hugging him tightly, I was weeping like a child. I had to leave once more.

It would take an entire day to travel to my new house. I was to be left alone to embark upon a new phase of my life, in an entirely different place, among entirely different people. Upon entering his room the first night and hinging up the door, he was surprised to find his new bride sitting on the floor in one corner, her back turned toward him.

"What are you doing?" he asked.

I was making sure my veena had withstood the long journey without any harm. Embarrassed, I put it back inside the box hurriedly.

"Is that your veena?" he inquired. "I am told you play this."

I nodded shyly, hoping dearly he liked music and would ask me to play. But he showed no interest at all. Instead he called me to bed. Awkwardly, we talked for a while and he sensed my hesitation. I understood then and there our worlds were vastly different.

My in-laws were traders. They had a distributorship, supplying grain to shops in the town and adjoining villages. Their business was thriving. My husband assisted his father in running the shop. He was a soft-spoken man.

I asked if he would like to hear me play. He said yes, reluctantly. I brought my veena to bed and played a short song, not forgetting to boast before I started that it was my father who had written the composition. He began to listen with interest. But as I proceeded, his energy waned, and he rested his head on the pillow. Midway through the song, my concentration was broken by a foreign sound. I opened my eyes to find him snoring with his mouth open. I sighed and continued. Never leave a composition unfinished, Father had taught us.

All was not doom. My husband turned out to be a good man with a gentle heart. And he was hardworking; he never shied away from responsibilities, nor was he imposing. I could not blame him for not being able to appreciate my music. Classical music is such that you can't just fall in love with it; the ears need to be trained from an early age for one to be able to appreciate it. I was lucky, and he was not. The fact that he let me live with my music without imposing any severe restrictions was enough for me to be grateful to him. But the journey had gotten lonely, very lonely.

A practical problem arose when it came to my early morning practice. I could not possibly play in our room at such an early hour without waking up my husband, who was a late riser. Neither could I go to any other room, even if one had been vacant. I needed my mother-in-law's permission for that, which I was frightened to ask for, considering her lukewarm attitude toward me. I could go to the veranda and play, but if someone noticed, it would be a disgrace for the family.

At the same time there was no way I would stop my morning practice, not even for a single day. So while the rest of the family slept, I tiptoed in the darkness, carrying my veena. I sneaked out of our room and out of the main house and into the cowshed that stood in one corner of the courtyard. I was a farm girl, so the presence of cows did not bother me. I sat comfortably on the haystack and played. I did not play for long and always went back home before the sun rose. I did not disturb the cows. Though they must have been surprised, my bovine audience seemed to enjoy my renditions. Fortunately my mother-in-law was still asleep when I returned. Waking up, she found me in the kitchen looking for utensils to boil the fresh milk I had milked from my audience as a fee for my recital. She was pleased.

It did not take long for my cowshed practices to get noticed. My husband woke up early one morning to drink some water, and not finding me beside him, searched the house. Not finding me anywhere, he feared I had fled to my village. Coming out, he heard string sounds coming from the cowshed. He had a chuckle seeing me playing, sitting on a haystack. More fearful than embarrassed, I pleaded with him not to tell his mother, which fortunately he did not. But he did tell her to allot a vacant room for me. Despite her reluctance, she did. From then on I practiced in that room without disturbing the rest of the family.

I gave my mother-in-law little opportunity to complain about housework. I was at her beck and call, doing everything that was expected of a dutiful housewife, even massaging her feet and the feet of my father-in-law every night before they went to sleep. Despite my efforts, she did not even try to warm up to me and would never spare an opportunity to criticize me, finding fault with my work even if there were no faults to be found. The reason was obvious. She did not take well my resolve to stick to my music. To lessen her resentment, I limited my practice to only an hour in the morning and half an hour in the evening.

Yet she remained aloof with me. I was doing something in her domain without taking into account her opinion. My husband was afraid of his mother. He tried to make her accept my passion, and when he wasn't able to do that, he tried to talk me out of it. But I made my stand clear. I was willing to compromise on everything but my music. If they did not allow me to play, I would leave them for good, whatever the consequences.

An uneasy truce prevailed between me and my mother-in-law. Despite her sometimes bitter, sometimes sugar-coated jabs, mostly centered around my family and our attachment to music, I continued with my practice in the solitude of what I now considered my room of solace. During the evening sessions, I would drown all the degradation and humiliation of the day with the sadness springing from my heart, longing for what I had lost or left behind. In the mornings I would start afresh, at peace with myself and the world, filling my heart once again with joy. Looking forward to a new day. But there were occasions when music could not provide solace, and I would cry silently, turning my face to the wall. My husband would try to console me. I felt sorry for him at times. There was nothing much he could do. It is not easy for a man to stand up to his mother.

I eagerly awaited letters from home. When the bell rang, announcing the arrival of the postman in our lane, I would rush to the door. Either he would run past, shaking his head, or he would stop with a big smile, delivering my letter. Father wrote mostly in his bold handwriting, sending me his compositions, providing beautiful words of encouragement, and valuable insights on the technical and aesthetic aspects of the different ragas. Mother, in her unstructured feminine handwriting, would add a few lines giving me advice on cooking and other aspects of running the household, never forgetting to remind me that I should be a good wife and an even better daughter-in-law. Taking care of my husband's parents should be my first priority. Murali, too, would add a few lines. I would respond with what they wanted to hear, not what was true. I wrote that I was happy in my new house with my husband and especially my mother-in-law treating me so well, letting me practice my veena as much I wished.

My relationship with my husband didn't seem to flourish since we had nothing to bond us except mundane, uninspiring, everyday communication. I became more and more withdrawn; however, I tried not to. For his part, he blamed me for being too attached to my family for my growing indifference toward him. He might have been right. I figured that having a child together could soften whatever resentment was growing in him.

***

With our child coming, my body became heavier, my appetite changed and my mood oscillated. At times my heart flooded, thinking about the life growing inside me. Feeling him moving inside my belly, I could not wait to bring him to the world. But there were times when I wondered whether he should be coming at all to a home where art was not appreciated, where his mother had to live a life over which she had little control. As my mind wandered into such lows, I would fall into a daze of depression. Then again, uplifted by a great sense of responsibility toward my yet-to-be-born. I decided I wanted to develop the child's musical sense while he was still in my womb, the way my musical sense had been developed. Mother told us Father played the veena dutifully before her every time she was pregnant, so that we could hear him and begin to appreciate music even before we were born. I wanted to do the same.

But however I wished, deep down I knew it would not be possible for me to pass on my art to my offspring in this bleak house. My Mother had my Father and Father had Mother. I had no one. My husband was a kind man, and with the child coming, he had been warmer toward me. I knew he would be a loving father, but I also sensed I would not have him by my side when it came to the question of raising our child. He would side with his mother instead. My mother-in-law was already laying her claim on her grandchild, having decided to name him after her own father, having no doubt whatsoever I would give birth to a boy and not a girl. I knew I was going to lose my child to her.

I wanted to go to my parents home and give birth there as most girls did, but when the proposal was not forthcoming from Father or Mother when I told them I was pregnant, I had an uneasy feeling things had changed back home. Mother had stopped writing. Father's letters had become formal; he rarely mentioned my brothers. I convinced myself that even if a proposal had come, my mother-in-law would have rejected it. This gave me some solace.

I gave birth on a cold winter night. He was so small at first, and so light. My heart flooded, taking him in my hands. Beholding his half-closed eyes, the little nose, the quivering lips, hearing his demanding cries, seeing the helpless movements of his limbs, I felt joy like never before. When he suckled from my breasts, a sweet feeling of warmth filled my body. The world seemed so beautiful. Even my overbearing mother-in-law did not seem hostile anymore. For a short period of time, we buried our hatchet and became friendly to each other for the sake of the newborn.

My son began to grow, filling my days and nights with so many pleasures and frequent concerns. His antics made me laugh; his cries made me rush. He demanded all my time, occupied all my thoughts. There was no question of continuing my veena practice in those early days of motherhood. Or feeling bad about abandoning it.

He was named Nand, after a night raga, as he was born as the moon gleamed.

My family was invited for the baby's first rice eating ceremony. Mother and Father came. I was so happy to see them, but I was equally appalled. How my mother had changed! She had grown old and thin, her hair had turned grey, and circles had appeared under her eyes. Father too, had grown older and weaker. His large frame shrunken, the mustache greyed, much of his hair was gone. I would have cried had it not been for my son. Mother told me what I had long suspected. Murali was now fighting Jatin over his share of profits from the land. The ongoing feud had taken a toll on Father. But seeing his two sons quarreling before his eyes and being able to do nothing about it, he had become so melancholy.

We did not talk music. Father did not ask if I was practicing or not. The baby took all his attention. Before leaving, he blessed me saying, "Don't give up" into my ear. I wanted to say the same to him. I felt so sorry for him, for myself, for all of us. There we had been, only a year ago, all together, leading our lives so happily. Now we were so far from each other, in every sense of the word, each with his own struggles, disowning music, or struggling to hold on to it.

The months flew by. Nand grew with every passing day. Soon he was crawling all over the house, trying to speak in his baby twaddle. Since he no longer needed my full attention and since I was not fighting his grandmother's scheme to appropriate him, I finally resolved to take to my veena again. But my mother-in-law now had other plans. Once again she returned to her old self, more determined than ever to dissuade me from my music. She began using my little one against me. At other times she would keep Nand to herself, not letting him come to me except at feeding time or when she was exhausted. But whenever I sat with my veena, she would send him to my music room. How could I play with the little one crawling up my veena, touching the frets and strings and everything shiny, beaming with the joy of discovery? Giving up practice, I would watch his antics with great joy, my passion taking a back seat to my motherly instinct. Let him grow some more, I would tell myself, then the two of us will sit together and I will play and he will listen, as we had listened to our father playing. The more he would listen, the more his ears would learn to appreciate and then a day would come when I would initiate him into my art, passing on to him the legacy of our father.

But my dream turned out to be a mirage. Every time I wanted to make it real, it slipped away. My motherly responsibilities, coupled with my household duties, took me further and further away from my veena. Bogged down by work, I would not go to the music room for days, then weeks, and then a whole month would pass without me touching my veena. Inspired at times by Father's letters—which were now just a trickle—I did try to practice, but with so much on my mind and my body so exhausted, I could not play as before. My inability to concentrate frustrated me. Irked at myself and the world, I would give up, locking the veena in its box. Months passed like this. Then finally, one day, I decided it was over. Convincing myself that my priorities had changed, I packed my veena up for good, and with it the great necessity of passing on my art to my son that I had once felt so passionately. I put both to rest in the darkness of the box and shoved it deep under the bed so that I did not have to see it when I entered the room.

The world had claimed me. I had become a true housewife and mother and a daughter-in-law, with no strings attached to me anymore. Looking after my child and husband was now the sole occupation of my life. And my mission was to bring up my son the way his father and grandparents wanted me to: a trader like them, carrying forward the family business, buying and selling commodities and counting profits. Then we would marry him to a pretty, homely girl, not saying no to dowry, on the contrary, demanding it. And then I would become a mother-in-law, no less overbearing than my own, making life difficult for my daughter-in-law as it had been for me. Life would come full circle.

It would have, had it not been for an incident that changed my life all over again.

7

A FINAL REUNION

Three and a half years had passed since I'd become a mother. Nand was now a curious little boy, running all around the house on his fresh legs, speaking clearly in his child voice, inquiring about every new thing his eyes picked up. I was nearing twenty-four, still young in age, but older in heart and in appearance. Motherhood and the incessant grinding of the family mill had taken its toll on me. My husband had been busy, too. Our business was booming as we supplied commodities to more and more retailers. Our packed daily schedules left us with little time to think of anything but our work. Since our marriage, we had been out only a few times. Each year a fair was held in a large space not far from our house during the ten days of Navaratri. Like all other people in town, we had been there, scanning the stalls, shopping and eating, and returning home after watching dramas based on mythical stories—the main attraction of the fair.

This year we brought our little one with us. It was the second day of the festival. Nand was so excited. He wanted to be everywhere at the same time, wanted us to take him to every stall, buy him every toy. The sun had set, people milled around in groups, and more were coming; the stalls and tents were lighting up with lantern lights. Nand, candy stick in hand, pointed at the Ferris wheel.

"I want to ride that," he pleaded.

I stopped, looking at his father.

"No, you won't," his father said firmly and, taking him from me, headed in another direction. We followed. I was unable to suppress my smile. I loved riding the Ferris wheel. I had never missed the opportunity every time I went to a fair. The previous year we had ridden it together, Nand's father for the first time. He was always scared of riding the Ferris wheel, and had boarded solely because I insisted. The first time around he had grasped my hand. And as the wheel picked up speed, he had begun screaming like a child, pleading the handlers to stop. They slowed it down and took him off. I did not get down. I went on riding till the finish, enjoying it to the hilt.

We came to a tent inside which a puppet show was about to begin. Nand's father bought the tickets. We were about to enter the tent when I heard a sound. A shiver went down my body. It was very faint and unclear amidst the din, but my ears did not fail to recognize it. Someone was playing on the veena. It was a composition composed by my father.

My legs barely moved as I followed my husband and mother-in-law into the tent. We sat on the carpeted ground waiting for the show to begin. My mind was in turmoil. It could not be Father; someone else was playing. Whoever he was, from what I'd heard in those brief moments, he was playing it very well. The show was about to begin but I could not keep sitting. "I need some fresh air," I whispered to my mother-in-law and came out of the tent. It was so noisy outside. My ears took a while to pick up the sound again. I followed it, making my way through the crowd.

By the time I reached the tent, the performance was over. A small banner stuck outside announced the name of the group: Bharat Sangeet. I entered with a thumping heart. Not many people were inside. An audience of twenty or so men sat before a stage on which five men sat in a semicircle fine-tuning their instruments. In the middle was the veena player, a handsome man in his mid-twenties, with a beard and curly locks that reached to his shoulders. On his right side was the mridangam player and on the left the tanpura player, both young men in their early twenties. A slightly older man sat beside the mridangam player; he had no instrument before him. Beside the tanpura player sat a young lad. He, too, had nothing before him.

I was the only woman inside the tent, and everybody was looking at me, including the musicians. I scanned the faces in the audience, fearful I might find a familiar one. I recognized no one, but was not sure if anybody recognized me. There were men who whispered to each other, looking at me. I thought of getting out, but my legs wouldn't let me. I sat on the ground, not going further in. The veena player began the next kriti.

He played it so well, exploring the various phases of raga Shankarabaranam with intense vigor and vibrancy, handling the swara patterns with such delicacy and deftness. I listened, enthralled, forgetting that only a few yards away my family sat in another tent and I should be there too. As he finished the kriti and the audience applauded, I came back to my senses and got up, suppressing my urge to know who these people were. I had taken a few steps out of the tent when a voice called from behind, "Sister."

I turned. It was the vainika. He had followed me out. The man smiled and said, "It was an honor to have you listen to our music, sister. Rarely do we have women in our audience. And you are the first without being accompanied by a man."

I did not know what to say. "You were listening so intently," the man continued. "I can tell you have an excellent understanding of music."

The compliment coming from a complete stranger embarrassed me. Nand's father must be looking for me; he might spot me at any moment. Yet I could not hold myself back. "Well, yes, I play the veena too," I said, blushing.

"You do?" The man was surprised.

"I am the daughter of Pandit Srinvas Iyengar," I could not help saying. It was Father's song the man was playing when I first heard him.

The man looked at me speechless. Then he said, "Why don't you play for us, Sister? It will be an honor to listen to you."

Now I stood speechless. I was a married woman and a mother. My husband, my son, and my mother-in-law were in the fairground and they must be looking for me. Given the situation, it was a proposal that could be termed nothing but sacrilegious. I should have politely refused, excused myself and walked away. But I found myself unable to do any of that. Instead I mumbled. "I… I… I don't know … I haven't played for a long while."

The man smiled and said, "Nothing can stop a true vainika from performing, Sister. Come."

I could have said I was an amateur, explained that I had never played in front of an audience before. But I did not. A compulsion beyond my control made me oblivious to the reality around me. My heart beating like mad, I followed the man into the tent, and then onto the stage.

"May I know your name, Sister?" the vainika asked.

I told him my name. The vainika turned to the audience and said, "Gentlemen, now our sister Leela Iyengar will play the veena for you."

I had told him my name was Leela Dharawadkar. But he introduced me with my father's surname.

I sat before the veena, numb with dread yet trembling with excitement. Everything around me seemed so surreal. The stage, the fellow instrumentalists who were all strangers, the vainika whose name I did not know yet, the audience… Feeling as if I were inside a dream, I bowed to the audience with folded hands, remembered the goddess, and asked my father to bless me. Then I began to play.

I played a short kriti based on raga Poorvikalyani composed by who else but Father. My out-of-practice fingers did not betray me. They moved up and down the frets and tugged on the strings as they always had, and in no time I became immersed in the reverberations. When I finished and opened my eyes, the audience had already burst into thunderous applause. I did not have the opportunity to savor the first public ovation of my life. Nand's father was standing at the tent entrance, his face dark as a thundercloud.

What followed was a torturous spell of dressing down by Nand's father and his mother. My parents, my love for music, my upbringing—everything was brought into question. My father-in-law did not say anything, but his grim silence was more menacing than the verbal reprimand. He would not let me serve his food. Nand's father would not sleep in the same room with me. Nand was not allowed to come near me. I slept alone in the music room.

It was so painful. I cannot explain how it feels to remain separated from your child. Hearing Nand cry, wanting to come to his mother, I wanted to die. Yet, in spite of all the humiliation and punishment, I could not hate myself for what I had done. On the contrary, a strange sense of accomplishment made me proud of my folly. I imagined Father in that audience, and Jatin. How proud they would have been to see their disciple perform and receive applause for it.

I was fortunate. After two days, Nand's grandmother exhausted herself looking after him; he was allowed to sleep with me during the night. But during the day she wouldn't let him come to me, unless there was no other alternative. One morning, while I was working alone in the kitchen, Nand sneaked in and tugged my sari end. After handing me a folded envelope and whispering, "A man told me to give it to you." He slipped away as quietly as he'd come. Locking myself in the music room, I opened the envelope. A letter was inside, written in clear, bold handwriting. I have read it so many times that even today I know every word by heart. This is how it went:

"Dear Sister, I am Vishnu Shankar, one of the members of Bharat Sangeet. It is upon my request that you played the veena that evening. It was not very difficult for me to find out where you live, as some in the audience recognized you and your husband. And it is not difficult for me to imagine the hardship you are going through because of what I made you do. For that I ask your forgiveness, if it is at all possible. I just want to tell you that you are not only a very good vainika and a true disciple of your revered father, you are also an extremely courageous woman. It is not easy for a woman in our country to follow her heart and accomplish things. You did exactly that. My colleagues and I are impressed beyond belief. We are a music troupe that travels around the country in an effort to bring to our people the treasures of carnatic music that in recent years have been under severe attack from the British rulers. The court of Mysore, which was the chief patron of carnatic music for centuries, has stopped doing so under pressure from our new masters. Many other patrons have followed suit, but fortunately not all. There are still many admirers, but afraid of British repression, they have stopped patronizing carnatic music overtly. For those connoisseurs and for many other lovers of our music scattered around the country

and, most of all, for the sake of keeping our rich musical tradition alive, we travel from one place to another, organizing recitals in small towns and villages, away from the glare of the British rulers who seem determined to destroy the treasure we value more than our lives. We have two vocalists in our group, one tanpura and one mridangam player. I am the only vainika. It will be an honor to have you as our first female companion. I know my proposal will shock you to no end. You are not only a wife but a mother too. You have responsibilities. Yet I give you this offer. If one day the urge to carry forward the legacy of your father surpasses all other urges you have within you, you can join us in our endeavor."

He gave an address where I could inquire about the whereabouts of the troupe and ended with an elegant signature.

The letter made me delirious. I forgot my pain, my humiliation, my degradation. In a state of frenzied excitement, I continued with my housework. My mother-in-law glanced at me cynically, as did my husband, but they did not bother me any longer. Getting an opportunity, I grasped Nand and hugged him for a long while. He did not utter a word, my boy. Little he might know but he knew his mother was in turmoil.

***

In the middle of the night, I pulled my veena box from under the bed. Taking out the even, I sat with it on my lap. I didn't play, only sat looking at it, grazing my fingers over it. I sat for a long time, then rose to write a letter. A long one.

Taking advantage of my mother-in-law's midday sleep, I slipped out of the house, drawing my sari to cover my face. Posting the letter, I came back as discreetly as I had gone out.

The days that followed passed in nail-biting anticipation. What if the letter failed to reach its intended audience? What if his response failed to reach me? What if he said no? Oscillating between soaring hope and mind-wrecking apprehension, unable to concentrate on my chores, inviting more wrath from my husband and his mother, I counted the days. Then one afternoon as I rushed to the door hearing the ringing of the postman's bell, he flashed me that broad smile of his and handed me what I waited for. Hiding it in my sari fold, I went to my music room. Locking myself up, I opened the envelope. Father had not written much. Only three words: Follow your truth.

I should have been filled with joy, having gotten the approval I was so eagerly waiting for. But I could not. The words were not boldly written as they should have been. Instead they were childlike, written with a trembling hand.

I did not waste time. I had to reach home as soon as possible. The next time the postman came to our lane, I handed him a letter. It was for him. I asked for his help in taking me to my village. I knew he would help me.

Three days later, a bullock cart stopped in front of our house in the wee hours of the morning. My belongings I had packed in a tin suitcase I had brought from home. There was nothing much in it. Nand's clothes, his milk, and some dry food for the journey, and a few sari of mine. A little cash that I stole from my husband, I had slid into my blouse. I had no guilt about it, considering all the dowry money and most of the ornaments I'd received from my parents that I was leaving with my in-laws. I lifted my sleeping boy in my arms, picked up the suitcase, and slipped out of the house. The postman's youngest son was waiting for me. He would be accompanying me on my journey home. He took Nand and the box from me. I went back into the house. There was no way I would leave without my veena.

I finally reached home. It was early morning. I saw Mother coming out of the bigger of the two huts in one corner of the compound that had not been there before. She was astonished to see us, then came running and took Nand from my arms. My heart sank looking at her. She had gotten older, the circles under her eyes deeper.

"What are these huts for, Mother?" I asked.

She did not answer, smiled, and took us in. I saw Father lying on a bed in one corner of the room. I felt numb. My father, the strong, handsome man who could take on the world single-handed, was now half the man he used to be. Wasted, with a grey beard covering his shrunken face, he was sleeping with his mouth open. As if he were dead.

Mother woke him up. "Look who has come!"

Father opened his eyes. He was confused for a moment, then noticed me and smiled. I threw myself on his chest.

They had not told me anything. Had not told me Father was sick. Had not told me the house was now truly divided. Before things could get any worse, Father had divided the property, including the farm, between Murali and Jatin. Murali now worked separately, lived separately, dividing the rooms and the kitchen between them. Not wanting to take sides, Father had built this hut for him and Mother. He had built a kitchen, too, for Mother, but fortunately the daughters-in-law still had the heart to feed the old couple. They brought the meals, one in the day, the other in the night. Mother did not have to cook. So much had happened and I did not know a thing.

"There is nothing left for you," Father said, holding my hand.

I smiled and said, "You have left your greatest treasure for me."

It did not take much time for grandpa and grandson to become the best of friends. "He is smiling after a long time," Mother said to me. Murali came to see me, separately, with his wife. Murali and Jatin had children of their own. I went to their respective homes, but only to pay a visit. Mother and Father had only one room but I stayed with them, sleeping on the floor with my son.

My priorities changed. Seeing Father in his sick bed, I brushed aside my desire to join the troupe. Taking charge from Mother, I began to look after him. I took him out to the verandah, messaged him with oil under the sun, took him to the bathroom, gave him a bath, fed him his medicines, and when he felt too weak to lift his hand, I fed him the food.

The first thing he asked of me was to play. He himself had stopped long ago. I played whenever he wished to listen, all the ragas he wished to listen to, as long as he wished, or until he fell asleep. As he listened, he would smile at me occasionally, nodding his head in appreciation of a well-executed alap, or a clever rendition of a tanam.

Three days after my arrival, he brought up the subject himself. "I had heard about the troupe before you wrote," he said one evening, after listening to my recital. "They are doing good work, very valuable work. It is your destiny that you met them. It is your life's calling. Write to them."

I told Father I did not want to go with them, leaving him and Mother.

Father smiled and said, "Tell them to come here. I want to meet them."

I wrote to the address mentioned in the letter. They received it and, canceling a program in another district, came to our place much more quickly than I had expected. All five came. Apart from the vainika—there was Adinath Chandrasekhara, one of the two vocalists, with a big shiny bald pate and a happy face. Narayan Daasanaanavar was the other vocalist. He was about the same age as me, slender with a thin moustache. Baladitya Mayachari, the mridangam player and Dayanidi Ishwar, the tanpura player, were in stark contrast to each other. Baladitya was large and grim-faced with unkempt hair and moustache, while Dayanidhi was soft, slender and fun-loving, clean-shaven, and impeccably groomed. They were so excited to meet Father and so respectful to him, as if he were a legend who had blessed their lives by meeting them.

Father was so happy in their company. Forgetting his sickness, he inquired about them, wanted to know about their musical quests, their understanding of music. As we sat on the floor before Father and talked, I felt I had known them for ages. They were family. Father asked them to stay for a few days, and they readily agreed. Accommodation did not prove to be a problem. Murali opened his doors to our new friends, since music and the presence of his little sister had brought us closer again, even for a brief period. They, too, sat with us in the evenings as we talked and played and sang, and after dinner, with the children gone to sleep, their wives would join us too. Those few days our house was transformed into a music academy where we all bathed and basked in the resonance of the ragas, forgetting our petty worldly differences.

Then one evening, accompanied by Murali, I played the first ever composition Father had ever composed, way back in his early youth. As he listened, half lying on his bed, ruffling my boy's hair, with Mother fanning him, sitting by his side, a smile spread across his face. After a while, he rested his head on the pillow and closed his eyes, not to wake up ever again.

8

THE PECULIAR LESSON

The days of mourning were over, it was time for me to leave. Mother did not try to stop me. Father had talked to her, telling her not to hold me back. Her concern about her grandson was large, though, and she urged me to leave Nand with her. I was touched by her generosity, but I could not leave without my child. Vishnu assured my mother. "We will bring him up together," he told them. "We are all educated people; we will take care of him, imparting our knowledge to him. He will not be found wanting." The words assured me more than anyone else. My son and I were in safe hands.

"Our doors will always be open to you. You can come back anytime you wish," my mother told me. That was no less reassuring.

So I left with my new colleagues, friends, and companions, embarking upon a new chapter in my life, with my little son in tow.

We were nomads. We played in secret. We relied on word of mouth to draw people to us, and hoped they did not draw the authorities who had forbidden us from playing. We did not know what would happen were the wrong people to catch us doing our work. We would be sent to prison, we imagined. We would be forced into hard labor. We had all heard rumors of what became of those who transgressed against our occupying army. My eyes scanned every sparse audience for a British uniform.

We spent months traveling from place to place. I was constantly in the company of others, and yet I was constantly apart from them. Nand needed frequent attention, and I admit, I was rarely willing to separate from him. Only during our performances did I let him out of my sight, and only because I had no choice.

The months were full of concerts at private homes crowded with listeners sipping tea, and out in the country on obscure, makeshift stages, where we had only a few spectators, sometimes whoever could be bothered to make the journey to see and hear us.

We got by, while we could, until at last our tour was brought to a halt by the eager, blue-eyed Sergeant Lacey, officer of the British army.

We had debated among ourselves, the question of whether the British even cared enough to enforce their new rules. If they caught us playing, would they arrest us? Would we be worth the trouble?

The sergeant seemed to think we were worth the trouble. He came to us at a house on the outskirts of the village. We were playing for a wedding celebration. I didn't see Lacey arrive. One moment he wasn't there, the next I looked and saw him standing with an unsmiling soldier and another man watching us play.

He waited until the performance was over, and when we were through, he approached at once, greeting Vishnu with a warmth that struck me as cruel. I felt certain he would place us under arrest. I thought he was taking joy in our misfortune.

The third man, I realized, was his interpreter. I heard him say the sergeant worked for a Colonel Hopkins.

I thought that I needed to find my son at once, and flee. I thought it was all over.

I found Nand playing with some other children. "Come with me," I said. "We need to hurry."

But when I glanced back, it was clear to me that no one was being arrested.

My fellow musicians exchanged confused glances. The interpreter was speaking—I couldn't hear what he said—while the sergeant continued smiling broadly. It was not a triumphant expression, I realized. He looked grateful.

The sergeant nodded, turned, and left with his interpreter, a shadow of a man who lifted his eyes only once, when he seemed to apologize to us with his expression as he turned away.

I rejoined the others and learned that we had been invited to see Hopkins, the colonel. He was stationed not far from there. The sergeant had learned we were nearby, and sought us out. A proposition was to be made.

"I don't like this," said Baladitya, shaking his head. "We shouldn't go."

"We have to go," said Dayanidhi. "We have no choice. If we don't go, they will lock us up for certain."

He was right, of course, and we all knew it.

We went to see the colonel, journeying a day to his provincial office. It was in a mansion at the heart of the estate of a wealthy family that had been displaced when the British arrived and repurposed their home. We did not enter the mansion. We gathered on the veranda, knowing we would not be allowed in. We waited an hour for the colonel to finish what Lacey called "urgent matters." We stood in our places, huddled together, until at last the sergeant, the colonel, and another man emerged. He was a new interpreter. There was no sign of the old one.

The colonel surveyed us with a cigarette hanging from his lips. His jacket was unbuttoned, his shirt open, revealing a pale, hairless chest. He was bald and clean-shaven. He must have been forty years old. He looked at us as if he had woken from a dream and thought he was still dreaming. His expression was that of a man who had fallen asleep in England and woken on that veranda far from home, not knowing quite where he was.

He spoke to Lacey. Lacey spoke to him. The interpreter did not translate. He did not, like his predecessor, apologize to us with his eyes. He seemed to rebuke us with them. His gaze was like a drawn sword.

The colonel gestured to us with a sweep of his hand and shook his head. His voice began to rise. I thought there must have been a misunderstanding. I thought this had gone all wrong. We would be arrested after all. Lacey spoke to his superior, and it seemed to me that he was pleading with him.

It was then that Nand tugged at my hand. I looked at him and he whispered something to me. I knelt so that I could hear him. He said he was hungry.

"Not now, child," I said. "This is important."

When I stood again, I looked and saw that the colonel was gone. Lacey was grinning again. He was telling us, the interpreter translating in a monotone, that we were being given an opportunity.

Sergeant Lacey, we learned, had been given the task of securing entertainment for some of his fellow officers. We were to perform for them. If our performance went well, and the officers were satisfied, more engagements would follow.

We would be, he said, emissaries of British culture. Just when I thought this sergeant had lost his head completely, he explained that we would perform for the officers and later for everyone who would listen to Western music. "Beethoven," he said, the translator repeating this name. "Mozart," he said, his translator echoing dutifully. He nodded and grinned. The translator swept his harsh gaze over us.

So, I thought. We are not to be arrested and jailed, but still, this is the end. Our days of playing music are over. Nand and I will return to his grandmother after all.

Lacey watched us, to survey our reaction. No one reacted. The smile left his face, and he instructed us to take a moment to discuss this among ourselves. He stepped inside, leaving us to decide our fates.

Nand must have sensed a change in the air pressure. As soon as Lacey was gone, he began to sing out a tune that Narayan had taught him some weeks before. He sang it louder than ever, this time, as he knew it was precisely what he should not do.

The others did not take notice. Their heated debate began at once. As they talked I took Nand in my arms, walked with him to the edge of the veranda, and squeezed him tightly. "Quiet," I told him. "Now is not the time." Moments later, I returned with Nand still in my arms.

"This is the only way for us to continue," I heard Dayanidhi say. "If we don't do this, we will have to go our separate ways. What will we do, then? It will all be over."

"It is over already," said Baladitya. "It was over the moment these British set foot in our province. It was only a matter of time."

"This is worse than being arrested," Adinath added. "Worse than having our instruments smashed to pieces."

"We will do as the man has asked," said Vishnu. Everyone turned to look at him. The debate had ended. It had not been a debate. As we all well knew, this was his decision to make.

After a silence, he said, "How long do you think these British will continue to live among us? Ten years? Twenty? One hundred years?" He shook his head. He looked around at us. "The music we play has survived far more, and far worse than this. We must continue our work."

"And play their music?" cried Baladitya. "That is no way to continue. That is our death."

"Calm yourself," said Adinath. "Our vainika is right. This is the only way."

And so it was decided. Lacey returned and grinned again when Vishnu told him how the matter had been settled. "Wonderful," he said. "Mr. Thompson will prove to be a capable teacher."

He saw the bewildered expressions on our faces. "You will need to be taught, of course," he said. "This is not a task for amateurs. Don't worry. Thompson is a capable man. He could teach an ape to play proper music. Now, go and rest up. There's work to do."

He left us then, and the translator ushered us away. He said we were to report in the morning to Thompson's office elsewhere on the estate.

As we left the office, Nand was cranky. He pulled at my clothes. Some of my fellows conferred with one another in low tones. I couldn't hear what they said.

British soldiers walked about, sweating in the afternoon heat. We passed the colonel, who reclined shirtless in a wicker chair, reading. A man stood by in a sarong, fanning him, while another buffed his toenails. The colonel's foot was planted firmly on his knee. His eyes were narrowed to slits. I thought he might have dozed off, where he sat. He did not look up at us as we passed.

Our translator escorted us to a barn. "You will sleep here," he said.

"What? In the barn?" said Baladitya.

He didn't respond.

"There is no sense in arguing," said Dayanidhi. "We will do as we must. At least there aren't many animals inside. Plenty of room for us."

The dissenters mumbled their discontent through the evening. I thought we might wake in the morning to find our numbers halved, our fellows disappearing in the night.

Instead, they talked through the night, Baladitya and Dayanidhi arguing over our predicament. They must have had as much trouble sleeping as I did, lying as I did with Nand in my arms listening.

"Empires have risen and fallen," I heard Dayanidhi say. "Nations have been ruined, and the music we play has not died. It's because of people like us, who have continued playing it, despite what has happened, despite things far worse than this."

"I don't know," said Baladitya.

"People have been brought into this world," insisted Dayanidhi, "and they have left it, to the sound of the songs we play. We must ensure that we are here when these people are gone. This is the only way for us to do that, to continue."

Baladitya was unconvinced. I was unconvinced. Nand sighed as his eyes shut, I kissed him on the head, and in the early hours of the morning, at last, I fell asleep.

***

I woke to the sound of someone urinating. I knew as I stirred from sleep what I was hearing.

Nand was gone. I stood at once, and looked around me. It was early morning. Nearly everyone was still asleep, as I stepped out of the barn in the growing light.

"Nand," I said. "Where are you, boy?"

"He's here," I heard Baladitya say.

I rushed around the corner of the barn to find Nand and Baladitya standing together, watching a man in a ragged uniform lean against the barn. His pants were undone. He had fallen asleep as he relieved himself.

I approached them quietly, not wanting to wake the sleeping man. "Come with me," I whispered to Nand. "Now."

Nand didn't move. "What happened to him?" he whispered.

"Nothing happened," said Baladitya. "That man is drunk."

I took Nand by the hand and led him away. To Baladitya, I said, "Come on, then. Our first lesson begins soon enough."

The lesson took place in a small house on the estate where, I gathered, our music teacher lived. We were led there by a young man—a boy, really—someone from the province who must have been drafted into service by the British from one of the nearby farms. He led us to an open room with a piano in it. There was just enough room for us all to sit and wait for the arrival of our teacher.

As soon as he entered, it was clear enough to me that he wasn't really a teacher, only an officer who knew how to play the piano. He had, I soon gathered, been assigned the task of teaching us based on this one qualification.

The first interpreter, the one we had encountered at the wedding, entered the room with Thompson. He was older than the colonel, and bald, like him. He did not walk in so much as stumble. He did not look at us until he stood and leaned against the piano. His eyes were pits. He seemed as if he hadn't slept in fourteen years.

"Welcome," he said quietly, the interpreter translating, also quietly. He sat down on the piano bench and lowered his eyes.

"That man is drunk," I heard Baladitya say. It was the second time I had heard him say it that morning. I thought at first he couldn't mean it, that he must be making a joke. As I watched the man, I realized he was making no joke. Our music teacher was drunk.

"I have been instructed to teach you to play music," said the man. "I'm afraid it won't be quite what you're accustomed to, but we will forge ahead. You might want to think of me as your guru."

He stressed that final word as if he found it difficult to utter the word. When he said it, I could not help glancing over at Vishnu to see his reaction.

He did not react. Like the others, he continued to watch Mr. Thompson.

"We'll start with Mozart," he said, and the translator began distributing among us papers he had held under one arm. It was sheet music. I suspected that we all knew what it was, but I knew for certain that none of us had any use for it.

All of us looked at the sheet music without expression. We must have all been mulling over the same question—how to explain that we didn't read sheet music without jeopardizing our arrangement. Whether we liked it or not, and we did not like it, we needed this man.

Mr. Thompson asked his translator an abrupt question. The translator mumbled something back to him. Mr. Thompson closed his eyes and put his hand on his forehead. He looked like he was in pain.

Those of us who sat there on the floor looked around at one another, until at last our teacher said, through the translator, "There has been a misunderstanding. We'll try it another way."

He turned away from us to face the piano. He played a melody that sounded simple enough to my ears. It went on for a couple of minutes. He played it slowly, perhaps so that we could catch its nuances. I had a distinct impression, it was far from the first time that I'd had it—that I, and my fellows, were being underestimated.

"Now," said Thompson, turning to us, "why don't you give that one a try?" He looked, for a moment, as if he was trying to smile. It seemed to hurt him to try to smile.

We gave it a try. We did our best. Dayanidhi played the melody our new guru had introduced to us, and repeated it as Baladitya joined him in accompaniment. On the next repetition, I joined them. As we played, I looked to Iyengar, attempting to read his expression. He watched us play as he did under other circumstances, his eyes closed for a moment, then open and alert, then back again in a steady pattern. I wanted to know what he made of this situation, of our playing for the satisfaction of someone who was an interloper. He must have never dreamed he would find himself there.

We played for a quarter of an hour. The melody we'd started with strayed until it became something else altogether, then returned and strayed and returned again. We added layers of texture and removed the layers as simply as we'd put them on.

It began to seem as if we could make something of the task that had been put before us—not that we would embrace it, but that it could work. When our performance ended, we looked up to our teacher who sat nodding gently to himself. He nodded for what felt like a long time.

When he was done nodding, he stood slowly and walked across the room. He opened the door he had come in through, and stepped over the threshold. He closed the door behind himself.

We waited several minutes, expecting him to return with more sheet music. He did not return.

Someone took a deep breath. Our translator stood, impassive, at the front of the room.

"Well?" said Baladitya, incensed. "What did he think? Did he like it?"

The translator looked back at him without expression. "I don't know," he said.

We never did know quite what our teacher thought of us and our playing, but on mornings that followed, we had more lessons. We learned more melodies. We knew, despite the detachment of the teacher we had been given, that we were making progress.

We had played for small audiences ever since I'd joined the troupe. Now we were playing for the satisfaction of one man. Strange as it was, we made the most of it.

We continued sleeping in the barn for several weeks. We ate what food the soldiers did not. We were made to wait until the last of them were gone before we were given food, to be taken to the barn and eaten there.

Most mornings, when we gathered for our lessons, our teacher was not there. We practiced what he had given us to learn. It was our translator who informed us of what we were expected to do. "I heard your teacher talking with that officer, Lacey. He expects you to obey the sheet music. Do as you were told, and no more." And so we taught ourselves to remain within the boundaries that were set before us.

On the morning of our final lesson, Sergeant Lacey came to see and hear us, standing to one side of the piano with a grin he could not seem to suppress. We played the compositions we had learned, works by Mozart and Strauss, with Adinath and Narayan joining us to sing Beethoven's "Ode to Joy." At the end of our performance, Lacey clapped his hands together and said, "You're ready."

He waited a moment, perhaps to see how we would react. We did not react, or know what he meant. "Your first performance is tonight," he said. "The officers and their wives will be dining in the camp. You will be the entertainment. I know you will not disappoint."

Still smiling, he left us sitting on the floor.

One of the servants came for us, as the sun began to go down. He led us, in our best clothes, our instruments in tow, to a stage they must have constructed in haste from planks that creaked and shifted as we walked across them. First Iyengar stepped onto it, followed by Adinath. It seemed the structure might well collapse under their feet. The rest of us stepped wearily aboard, one by one, the boards groaning.

"When we first came here," said Baladitya, "I thought they might kill us if we didn't do what they said. Now at least I know this stage will kill us no matter what we do."

But despite our fear of the boards under our feet, we set ourselves up. We tuned our instruments as the sun went down, and the servants lit torches beside the stage and surrounding the cloth-covered tables where our audience would sit.

We sat for an hour, waiting for them to come, mumbling among ourselves. Flies buzzed. Mosquitos sang in our ears. I wondered, as the others must have, when we would be asked to begin, and when we would have an audience.

At last they arrived, two by two, men and women paired together, the men sweating in their uniforms, the frowning women pale in the torchlight. We watched them sit at the tables, nodding and speaking to one another, one of them looking up at us on occasion, with an expression I could not read. They seemed to see us as if we sat behind a pane of glass, as if we were far away, seen through a telescope.

The servants, young men from the surrounding province, brought drinks for the men and women at their tables, at which time Sergeant Lacey emerged onto the stage, stepping across it with a self-assurance that unsettled me, for as his boots pounded the stage the boards shook underneath us. He spoke to the audience, who applauded him several times. There was no one to translate what he said, but at length he stepped aside and gestured to Vishnu, and we began to play the Mozart we had learned.

As I played, I caught glances of the crowd and saw that they behaved just as they did before we began. They talked to one another. They laughed and took long drinks from the glasses in their hands. They behaved as if the music they heard emerged from the landscape, and there were no players on the stage before them at all.

It was not until we were halfway through playing, at the start of our rendition of Beethoven's "Moonlight Sonata," that Vishnu announced in Hindi the names of the players. It was what he did at every performance, and as always I bowed my head when he spoke my name.

It was, of course, not only my name but my father's name, and when he spoke it, the servants, who had been busy fetching fresh drinks for the audience members, stopped and took notice. I caught glimpses of them as I began playing, of one and another of them taking the first looks at us that they had dared to take.

Some of the British they were waiting on looked around at them, and seemed to take their first notice of us as well. I was far from home, and we may have entered a world other than our own when we stepped onto that flimsy stage, but my father's name still meant something. That, to me, meant something.

When we were done with our "Ode to Joy," our Mozart, and our "Blue Danube," Sergeant Lacey reemerged with his grin and spoke to the small crowd, which had only grown smaller as members of the audience abandoned their places. The ones who were still present applauded him, and I understood, somehow, that the applause was meant for him, not us. Even the clapping of their hands did not translate to our ears. The remaining British left, and Sergeant Lacey turned to us, still grinning. The translator joined him at his side.

"That was excellent," he said. "I think they were amused, don't you?" He did not wait to hear a response. "I will draw up a schedule for your next performances," he said. "You'll be taking this show to certain far corners of the province. And when you do perform again, I'd like you to make things slightly more interesting. Act out scenes, you know?"

We sat in baffled silence. Finally, Vishnu said, "What kind of scenes?"

"Nothing complicated. Short plays, with clear morals." He must have expected us to express our understanding. We did not. "A husband is unfaithful to his wife," he explained. "And so she shouts at him, hits him on the head. Punch and Judy stuff, but for the local crowd."

"We'll work on it, all right? You will get your marching orders. For now, well done. 'Once more unto the breach, dear friends.'"

He walked away, and left us alone on the stage. No one spoke for a while. Eventually, we returned to the barn.

9

SILENCED

The next morning, we were told where to go, a town some hundred miles away, where we were expected to appear in two weeks' time. There was an outpost with half a dozen British soldiers stationed there, "To keep the locals in line," we were told, and we would keep them entertained for an evening.

So we set out, glad to be away from the music lessons and the sight of all the uniforms. When we were sent off, Vishnu was paid, we did not know how much, enough to keep us fed and sheltered as we traveled. He was given papers too, to indicate that we worked on behalf of the British army.

On the night of our first day traveling, Baladitya brought to our attention the time of year. We were approaching the Guru Purnima. "Surely," he said, "we can take the time to celebrate."

"Celebrate it how?" said Adinath. "Among ourselves? For us alone?"

"I know this area," said Baladitya. "Some years ago, I played at a celebration, a festival that was staged not far from here."

"Do you think they will still have it," I said, "given the rules that have been put in place? Surely they would not hold it, given the potential for retribution."

"We are not in a city, Leela," he said. "We are far from the authorities. It is out here in the farmland that they insist on upholding tradition."

And so, as much out of curiosity as determination, we stopped in a town halfway between our starting point and destination. Baladitya made inquiries and learned he had been correct. The festival would be smaller, surely, than in prior years. It would be quieter, but it would be held.

"What are we doing in this town?" asked Nand, looking around. "Where are we?"

"We are going to a festival," I said. "The Guru Purnima."

"What is that?"

"Has your mother not told you," asked Dayanidhi, "about the Guru Purnima?" He looked at me in mock consternation. "It is a festival in honor of our teacher. When we honor and celebrate him, without whom we would be nowhere."

"I think this is nowhere," said Nand.

When Baladitya learned the location of the festival, we traveled to where it would be held, some miles from the center of town on the grounds of a tea plantation. We arrived a day early, and we were welcomed by the few dozen who were there ahead of us. They would be honored, they said, if we would perform at their festival.

It was not much of a festival. Only a few dozen more attendees came to the celebration, throughout the evening than were there already. The sky, at least, was clear, so that the full moon shone brightly. We did not light torches for fear of attracting attention. Still, we attracted attention.

In the night, we performed for the small crowd of people who gathered around us. We played as we had before, growing more absorbed in our music as the night wore on. We grew so absorbed that we, or, at least, I, did not notice until it was far too late that soldiers from the British Indian army had come to stand on the edge of the crowd, their rifles glinting in the moonlight.

And what would I have done if I had seen them coming? There was nowhere for me to go. And when they came, I did not at first see them. I felt their presence there, like a shadow that had fallen over us, as if something had come between us and the moon above. I glanced up at the audience, and everyone stared forward but did not see us. They were frozen in place.

When the performance ended, a pale-faced man, a British officer who must have led the Indian soldiers there, asked those of us on the makeshift stage, "What is this about? You are aware this is an illegal assembly?"

He needed no translator. He did not speak English, but Hindi. He must have learned it from having lived among the troops he commanded. We had not heard a white man speak a language other than English. I was dumbfounded by the sound of it.

Vishnu spoke for us. "Sir," he said, holding out the papers Sergeant Lacey had given him. "We are allowed to perform. It has been ordered by the colonel."

The officer took his papers, leafed through them, and said, "These say nothing about what you're doing here. What are you doing here?"

I did not hear what Vishnu said. I was looking from one part of the crowd to another. I did not know where Nand had gone. I had to find him. I did not see him. I stood and tried to leave the stage, but one of the soldiers advanced on me, holding out his rifle, to push me back.

"My son," I said to him quietly. "I need to find him."

He shoved me back. I stumbled and nearly fell onto my veena. I looked at him in shock. I heard the officer issue orders to his troops. "Arrest them," he said. "All of them."

I shouted my son's name. He did not respond. "Have you seen him?" I asked Baladitya. But he was dragged away by two of the soldiers.

It took two of them to drag me away too, blind as I was with rage and fear. I remember that I cried out. I remember my feet being dragged across the grass. I do not remember what followed. I remember the cell they took me to where I was kept alone, day and night, and fed water and bread through a slot in the door. I remember the way it smelled there, unmistakably like urine. Like someone in the cell beside mine relieved himself on the floor in the night, so that the heat, when it rose in the morning, caused it to rise into the air around us, where it stayed until the night that followed.

They kept me I do not know how long. I thought someone would come to speak to me. For so long, no one came. Had it not been for the daily ration, if it could be called that, I would have thought I'd been forgotten.

There were scratch marks on the walls—left, I imagined, by men and women as they scraped with the nails of their fingers the stones that held them in. Over and over they scratched, until at last they left impressions. They scratched maddeningly, and were driven mad by the same sounds I heard, the weeping and praying, the howling and pleading.

I made up faces for those prisoners who'd come before me, invented lives they might have led. They were vagrants, beggars, and prostitutes. They were men who stole livestock, women who went mad and smothered their children.

I thought if they could have seen me there, they would have been amused at the sight of the daughter of a veena player who had thought she could play her father's instrument. She had thought she could keep it alive and continue his work, though he was gone. She thought she was destined for something other than this. I could not keep my father's instrument alive. I could not even keep it intact.

My father's veena was destroyed on the third day after I was remembered again by the men who had put me in that cell and forgotten me. When I was brought to mind again, I was brought before a red-faced British man in a rumpled uniform. I do not recall the man's name, though I saw him many times. I was taken to him twice a day. It was never clear why. He never asked me questions, though he said many things. He shouted them in my face.

There was sometimes an interpreter present. More often, there was not. I knew, when his words were translated for me, that he wanted me to know I would die there. He thought I was no better than a whore. I learned certain English words from the way he repeated them, words I will not repeat for how foul they sounded spilling from his mouth.

I thought, for my first two days of this, that he must not have known why I was there at all. He must have thought I truly was a prostitute from how he spoke to me. He must have confused me with someone else. Then, on the third day, he brought in my father's veena. My heart broke when I saw it in that place.

He asked me, through the interpreter, to play. And I did play. For an hour,

I filled that prison with sounds the likes of which it had no doubt not heard before. For the first time since I arrived, I heard no sounds emerge from other cells. All was silence, aside from the song of my lone instrument. I thought perhaps the red-faced man would let me play forever. And perhaps he would have. But I stopped, and when I stopped, he opened his eyes—I had not realized they were closed—and took the veena from my hands. He held it as if he were handling a sacred thing, a bird's egg, or a newborn child.

He dropped it on the stone floor. He brought his black boot down upon it, again and again, until it lay broken into pieces.

I did not look up at his face when he was done. I looked at his boot, and said, not for the first time, "Where is my son?"

"Your son is dead," he said, not for the first time.

I didn't believe him. I knew he was lying. I knew I would not see my son again, but I knew he was not dead.

I looked up at the man's face then to see him smiling. And it was not his smile that filled me with rage. It was how plainly he was trying not to smile. If his joy at the sight of my despair had been put on, I could have borne it. But I knew from his effort to keep his lips from curling upward that his glee was something real, something that elevated him. And that is why I raised my face to his.

He had stepped forward. He was mere inches from me. I spat in his eyes, reached my hands up, and clawed at him with the same fingernails I had used to trace the rivets in the stones that lined my cell walls. I did not tear the officer's eyes from his red face, as I had wanted to. The interpreter pulled me away. The officer fled the room, and I never saw him again.

I was forgotten again, for weeks or months, in that place where time meant nothing, where I baked in the heat of my cell until I was taken with my wrists in chains to another prison a hundred miles away.

With five others, to whom I did not speak, I was taken in a horse-drawn cage to the place that would be my new home. I knew from how the prisoners in the yard clamored to see the new arrivals that new arrivals rarely came. This was a forgotten place. I was forgotten. I felt certain that this time I would not be remembered.

10

A LOST SOUL

My memory of living in prison is hazy. In my first days, I lived in a fog that took a lifetime to clear. I did not want it to clear. I did not want to see the place where I was, did not want to see the guards I could hear shouting throughout the day, or see the face of the woman I heard moaning every night for her lost son. She moaned into the dark until she slept. It would echo through that prison until the last of us was gone.

I did not want to leave my bunk, flea-ridden though it was, not even to eat. And for days I did not leave it, except to relieve myself and, when thirst threatened to choke my throat, to bring a cup of dirty water to my lips. I would have died there, had I not been pulled away and convinced that I should live. A woman came to me the third morning I woke there. She brought me fresh water, and food, if it could be called that.

"Eat," she said. "You will not like it, but you must eat."

I ate. The woman said, "My name is Sarada." She said it was her duty to help women like me, who were in the shape I was in.

"They do not often arrive here like this," she said. "It usually takes at least a month for this to set in. And even then, they move their hands to brush off the fleas. I have not seen you do even that since they dropped you there."

I was finished eating. I was finished listening. I turned away and lay there I knew not how long.

"The food has gotten better since I arrived, so at least there is that," said Sarada.

I had thought she had gone. I had thought an hour had passed since she had last spoken. Sarada said, "The only problem is, with better food come larger roaches. Which is a good thing, if you like roaches."

I turned slowly back to the sound of her voice, and at last I opened my eyes. I saw that she was young, younger than I expected. As young as I was. She was looking back at me gravely. She took this task seriously, ushering me into the world we were trapped in. I lay there a long time, gazing into her eyes, until at last she said, "Now let's get up. Let me help you."

I leaned on Sarada as she led me out of the bunkhouse where I had lain for days. I stepped into the morning light. My eyes burned at the sight of it.

"It's all right," said Sarada. She helped me sit on the ground. I saw that I was beside a small cistern. I reached my hand out, for I was thirsty.

"Don't drink that!" Sarada cried, pulling my hand back. "That is not for drinking."

I turned to look at her, still squinting in the light. "What is it for?" I said.

"I am not telling you that," she said. "Not now."

"Why not?"

"Come on. Stand up."

"But what is the water for?"

"I need to show you where you will work."

"Work?"

I later learned that if Sarada had not stirred me, that day, the guards would have come for me themselves. Time was running out. They would have beaten me and then made me wash my blood from the stone floor. I saw it happen, later, to other women. I saw a guard posted against a wall, looking sleepy, a club hanging from his belt. I saw a stoop-shouldered old woman who seemed to struggle simply to walk. She was going in our direction to the workhouse.

"Most of the women here are prostitutes," said Sarada. "Nearly every woman here has had to sell her body. They had nothing else left to sell. They needed to eat. They had a child to feed, or three children, or four. Do you understand? They will never see their children again. They gave up everything for them."

I understood that by saying these things Sarada was either asking me about myself or telling me about herself. I soon learned that this was how such talk proceeded among inmates. No one wanted to admit what they had done. No one wanted to press others to do the same. Sarada never said outright what had brought her there, or what her life had been prior to her sentence there. These things were made plain through diagonal formulations.

She told me instead about the duration of her stay, and what she had done there, as if life had begun for us at that prison.

"I have been here three years," Sarada said, as we neared the workhouse. "I have found that it is best to behave. To do as they tell you to do."

"What do they tell you to do?" I asked.

"To work. To eat. To continue living, so that you may continue working."

We stepped together into the workhouse, where dozens of women sat in a row under the wooden roof on the floor, spinning wool. Some were younger than I was. Others were as old as my mother. Light poured in from the windows. A guard sat on a wooden chair, leaning against the wall, dozing. The air did not stir in there. It was hot. The room was silent, and when we entered no one seemed to notice we had come in.

Sarada spoke quietly, I did not know why. "You have done this before?" she said.

"No," I said. "I am a musician."

She suppressed a smile. "Of course you are. But now you spin wool. The guard will bring water on the hour. Make yourself useful. I will see you again."

I sat between two women, before a pile of wool and some wooden tools. I began to do my work with nothing to look forward to but the next drink of water.

I worked, ate, and slept, for days that became months, until the work was second nature to me, until I dreamed as I slept of the work I did when I was awake. I dreamed of work, and of my son.

I saw Sarada often. I learned about her only what she let me know: that she did not work spinning wool; she worked on behalf of the warden, keeping watch over her fellow inmates. She was given more food than the others, some of which she shared with me.

With all that I had lost, I had also lost the flesh on my bones. Sarada promised to restore it. "We will bring you back," she said, smiling in a way that would have been pretty, were she not missing her front teeth. "We will make a model prisoner of you yet."

Perhaps she should not have said such a thing. Perhaps with that statement, she cursed me.

It was on that day that I was first brought before the warden, whom I had not seen previously. I had seen only his guards, and had seen them everywhere: a dozen disheveled men with beards who grinned their mockery at us when we had to relieve ourselves under their watch.

On that day, the guard who was in charge of bringing water to the workhouse did not bring it. We toiled in silence for an hour, expecting the only relief we were afforded. It did not come. An hour later, once again, it did not come.

I heard murmurs go up around me when the water did not come. I heard the stirring of the women's discontent, for not only were we thirsty; the bringing of the water was how we marked time. It was how we knew the day was moving forward as it should; that time indeed passed; that we were not lost to this toil forever. We would someday move on and be free. All hope hinged on the passage of time.

When another hour passed without the guard bringing us water, the murmurs returned and grew louder. The guard dozed in the corner, still. There was no sign of the guard we expected. Something in me broke.

"Where is he?" I said, quietly at first.

"Where is he?" I said again, more loudly.

I shouted, "Where is our water?" and stood and marched toward the workhouse guard, who was awake now, with his club in his hand as though it had leapt there.

"Sit down," said the guard, shaking himself awake.

"I will sit," I said, coughing from thirst, "when I have had water to drink."

"You have water to drink when we bring you water."

"We have not had water all morning. Where is it? We are thirsty? We cannot work like this."

"You will sit down," he said, stepping forward.

"I will do nothing," I screamed, "until I am given water!"

His gaze did not leave my face as he jabbed me in the stomach with his club. I dropped to the ground, gasping for air, coughing through the dryness in my throat. I heard another woman moan at the sight of me. I heard the guard above me shouting for his fellows. I lay there, on the floor, and choked on my thirst until two men took me away.

I was brought to meet the warden for the first time. I looked him in the eyes as the guard announced me and the nature of my offense. The warden was a small man with a trimmed beard and eyes that seemed to have lives of their own. Even when he looked at me, his gaze flitted from my face to my bare feet and back. They darted always from one place to another. He sat behind his desk and said, "You have not been here long. Already you have made a commotion."

"I was not making a commotion," I said. "I was asking for water."

"She made demands," said the guard behind me. "Shouting and carrying on."

The warden regarded me coolly. "You are given a drink of water on the hour. That is more than enough."

"The water was not brought in," I said, before he finished. "For hours, we baked in that tent, without water."

The warden's gaze landed on the guard behind me and settled there for a long, discomfiting moment. The guard behind me must have nodded, or shrugged—something passed between the two men that amounted to understanding. Finally, the warden sniffed, nodded, and said, "Take her away." I was foolish enough to think I had been vindicated.

I knew better than to expect an apology, but surely, I thought, the warden realized a mistake had been made. The guard who had fallen asleep, or neglected his duties, would be punished. Order would be restored.

I was taken, instead, to a wooden box that stood alone in an obscure corner of the prison grounds. It was the size of an outhouse, and at first I thought that was what it was. But when I was shoved inside, I found it was merely an empty box, pitch dark and hot as an oven.

When the door shut behind me, I shouted at the guard who had put me inside. I demanded to know what this was. He did not respond. I slapped the door with my hand. It was locked tight.

I did not hear the guard leave, but once I had finally passed out from the heat I woke, hours later, to the sound of his return. By then I was curled up on the dirt floor of the box, which was not large enough to lie down in. I knew the sun had set, for the heat, which had sucked the waking life from me, had subsided.

When the guard swung the door open, my head, which had rested against it, spilled out onto the ground. The cool night air washed over my clothes, which were still damp from the sweat that had poured from my skin.

"Come on," said the guard. "Sit up."

He pulled me up and rested me against the outer wall of the box. He was far gentler with me than he had been; even such brutes as these men were must have been mollified by the sight of a half-broken woman. I watched him with my eyes half-closed as he brought a cup of water to my lips, and did it again and again until I shook my head, to tell him I had had enough.

"Come with me," he said, and lifted me from the ground. "Walk." And as we walked, he tried to explain things. "You must behave yourself," he said, as if I were an uncomprehending child. "Punishments like this will only get worse."

And so they did.

Some weeks later, the next time I was brought before the warden, it was for reprimanding the guard who was in charge of the latrine, which was nothing more than a shallow ditch over which we took turns squatting. This was the worst of every day's indignities, and the guards nearly always seemed to know it and disregard our dignity altogether. They made no effort to hide how they watched us, and one day I had simply had enough of it. As I took my turn urinating, I locked eyes with the young guard who watched me intently. I said, "Don't strain your eyes so hard. You'll go blind."

The punishment I was given, two days of hard labor, spent hammering rocks with a pickaxe, and reduced rations, was not enough to make me regret what I had said. I regretted that I could not summon words that would make that young man feel the shame he was missing.

My third visit to the warden was brought on by a coughing fit I suffered during work hours. I could not control it; it was hardly my fault; but that hardly mattered. By then, I was a marked woman. I understood that anything I did was bound to bring on consequences of one sort or another.

This time, I was returned to the wooden box and left there for two days, with only a short water break in the morning and evening. I felt certain this time that the box would be my coffin. The heat and my thirst combined to bring me visions of my father and mother, my departed son, and the troupe I had traveled with. It was dark as night in there, but I saw many things. And then, on the second night, as I lay on the edge of death, my body like a dried husk, I heard thunder. It began to rain. I was saved by the poor construction of the wooden box, which leaked rainwater onto my face, stirring me awake.

Soon it was pouring in the little chamber. I cupped my hands and drank.

"If you aren't careful," Sarada told me when I returned to the bunkhouse, "you will disappear."

For a moment, I thought she meant the box would swallow me up, that I would be swept away with the visions I had had, of my mother, father, and son.

She could see I did not understand.

"It is what happens to women like you," she said.

"Women like me?" I rasped, my voice strained by my prolonged thirst of the prior days.

"Those," she said, "who are taken to the warden too many times. They do not last long."

"The guards kill them?" I said.

"Not all. Some they take away to the colonies. To the islands." She could see I did not understand. "There are many prisons, Leela," she said. "They are not all just like this. There are whole islands that have been made prisons, colonies where men mix with women. Women are sent there and forced to marry the men and work the land."

"That is where women like me are sent?"

"Some are sent. Some choose to go. Don't look so surprised, Leela. Imagine knowing only prostitution from when you are young. A stable life, even a stable prison life, might look appealing then. And if you don't want to join them there, you will want to behave."

"Behave? All I did was cough."

"It doesn't matter. They have noticed you, Leela. You must make yourself invisible. Do all that you can to keep them from noticing."

"And if I can't do that?"

"Then prepare yourself for a long journey by sea. Or pray that you are taken from this place, somehow, some other way."

That night, I could not sleep. I did not pray. I did something not much different. I wrote a letter, in my head, to the nearest thing I knew to a god: the Maharaja. He was not as powerful as any gods I knew of, but I thought he would make a more likely ally, if I could only reach him.

11

THE SAVIOR

In the morning, as we sat on our bunks, I asked Sarada if she could retrieve some paper for me. I knew she had access to it, where she did her labors that were far lighter than what the rest of us did. Compared to the others, she spent her days in the lap of luxury.

"I will need something to write with too," I said, "though I can improvise that, if necessary." I would write with my blood if necessary.

"What is it for?" Sarada asked. She eyed me like I was a danger to myself. Perhaps I was.

I took a breath. "I need to write a letter. I will need you to send it. You can do that, can't you?"

She shook her head. "I couldn't," she said.

"You must," I said. "And I know you can. Messages must be sent from here to elsewhere. There must be a way."

"There is a way," she said. "But…"

"But what? If you don't do this, you know what will become of me. I'll die here. Or I'll be sent away, and die in exile, the wife of some thief or murderer."

"All right," sighed Sarada. "I will see what I can do. But I make no promises."

I wrote my letter. Sarada took it from me.

Three months passed. I spent three more nights in the wooden box, and five more days at hard labor as punishment for more offenses. The first offense was glancing at a guard as I accepted water from him; the second was falling asleep, out of sheer exhaustion from my prior punishment as I sat and worked among the other women; the third offense was coming down with an illness that took everything from my body that was left, and left me sprawling in the wooden box, nearly wishing for death.

I felt certain I would die there at last. They would punish me until I was dead, or until they chose to ship me away to a colony. I felt certain I would not survive the journey.

The door opened. The night poured in. I looked up with one eye to see not the guard gazing down at me but the warden himself, in his ragged nightwear, looking as small and wasted as I felt. I had not seen, before then, how frail he was, how small he was. He looked as if, in my healthier days, I could have broken him in half.

I watched him and panted what I thought were my last breaths. I thought he had come to watch me die. But instead he said, "You have a visitor." To a guard he turned and said, "Give her water. Clean her up."

I was given water, given food, and allowed to take a bath. I felt certain I would be shipped away that very day, that this was the end. My visitor must have been a boatman who would ferry me to my death. But instead I was led into a rather ornate room I had not seen, a prison lobby, I supposed.

The Maharaja was there, waiting.

I saw him before he saw me: he was looking around expectantly, with attendants on either side of him. Rifles were slung across their backs. They wore pistols on their belts. They were bodyguards. I had thought I might be dead, that my death was a dream. But when the Maharaja laid his eyes on me, I knew I was alive. I knew I would live.

Had I been dead, he would not have risen from his seat in a rage and charged at the warden, crying out that he should be shot for how I had been treated. I had not said a word; he must have seen in my emaciated frame all the evidence he needed of what they had done. I would have wept if I had tears left to weep, to see the warden sink to the floor and kowtow to the Maharaja, who had no title now, but was still regarded as if he were a monarch in certain corners of our world.

The Maharaja ordered one of his men to take me away, to where I did not know, and as soon as I was in his grip I fainted.

The days that ensued are obscure to me now. I slept for much of that time, and when I did not sleep I ate. I must have eaten more in those three days than I had eaten in three months.

It was the mangos I remember best. They tasted better to me than anything else I was given. I do not know why. I remember that when I ate them I felt as if I were eating for the first time.

I traveled alone for two days in a horse-drawn wagon. The first time we stopped, I asked the driver where the Maharaja was.

"He is coming," he said.

"Coming? But where?"

"In another wagon," said the man. "He sent us ahead."

"Ahead to where?"

"Where else? To the train station."

"What train station?"

The man laughed. "The one where the train stops. How else do you think he arrived here? Come on, climb back in. Eat up. You look like a skeleton."

There was a basket there with me, full of more food than I could eat in a week. I did as he said and put all of this together in my mind. Of course there was a railroad near the prison. How else could the Maharaja reach me in time to save my life?

The next time I saw the Maharaja was the first time I rode in a train car. I had been given new clothes to wear, and while I must have looked like death still, I felt restored to life. I did not know where I was going until he arrived in his private car, where I sat waiting for him.

He was tall and fit. He entered wearing a well fitted brown suit in the Western style and glasses. He walked with purpose, and you could tell he was no peasant. His bodyguard stood outside the door. I could see him through the window.

"Leela," he said.

My eyes began to well up with tears. I bowed, to hide them, and to show my respect. "Sir," I said.

"Please," he said, and sat across from me. He watched me as I looked out the window, at the countryside that seemed to speed past us.

"How things have changed," he finally said.

"We are very far from the palace," I managed to whisper in agreement. Tears streamed down my face.

"Why do you cry, Leela?" he said.

I blinked and looked at him. "I am sorry, I am very happy. I cannot express my gratitude to you."

"You need not express it," he said.

"You have restored me to life," I said. "Still I have nothing. My father is dead."

"I know, Leela."

"My son is…" I could not finish the thought.

"Your son is what?" said the Maharaja.

"I don't know," I said. "He was taken from me."

"Yes. To your mother."

"What?" The Maharaja smiled. "Your son is with your mother. That is where we're going. Did you not know?"

I couldn't speak. Of course I didn't know. "My son is…"

"He is waiting for you, Leela. He is waiting to see his mother."

"He knows I am coming?"

"Of course he does. I sent word. It will take you a few days to arrive. I will accompany you part of the way. You weren't told any of this?"

I shook my head. I could not speak. Tears bathed my face.

I was truly restored to life then: rescued from death by royalty, and returned to life by the need that someone, my own son, felt for me. I was not only moving in that train car toward the rest of my life. I was going home.

"I wanted to give you this," said the Maharaja. "I can only guess what became of your father's."

He pulled a sheet off of an object that had lain on the seat beside me. I had not thought to wonder what it was.

It was one of my father's veena. I could tell because of a unique crack that parallels the frets. The crack was made when I dropped it the very first time I played it. It was more ornate than I had remembered.

"This is for me?" I asked.

"Yes, it belongs to you," he said.

I reached over and touched it with my hand. I thought perhaps he would ask me to play it. And if he did, I would. But on that day, the Maharaja had brought two things to me: this instrument, and my son.

Epilogue

Leelavathi took a deep breath, pausing behind the curtain for a moment before continuing her slow walk onto the stage at the Mysore Palace. She exhaled, closing her eyes as unexpected emotions flooded her. Was she really about to perform in the place that held so much wonder for her as a girl? Her eyes misted, veiled momentarily in memory.

In her mind's eye, she saw the massive gate surrounding the palace, and recalled the sentries who first let her family pass through the gates into the beautiful, fragrant gardens of the palace itself. So many years had passed, yet she still recalled riding past manicured hedges and seeing a massive garden with gorgeous flowers everywhere. The palace's impressive arches and hundreds of windows surrounded a towering dome at the center the likes of which she had never seen.

Leelavathi remembered the day she witnessed her father perform in the durbar and the immense joy it brought. She could vividly recall the happiness that had sprung up inside her, and the pure beauty of the music streaming from his veena on that momentous day—the last time her father had ever performed at the palace.

As she had arrived at the palace tonight, now a grand concert hall, she had again been amazed by the beauty of the venue as it lit up against the darkening sky. A warm, lovely night during the month of guru purnima. She was quite pleased that this was an evening concert, primarily because it had given her time to prepare to perform in front of the largest crowd she had ever encountered in her career. She supposed she should be nervous, but she was much too old for that. She was resolved to make this, her final performance, the best it could be.

Although her hampered vision would make it difficult to see her loved ones in the crowd among the rest, she knew they would be applauding her; the ones in attendance and those who had passed. Several of her family members were there, and even some of her bandmates' descendants.

Dressed for the concert in a lovely blue patterned sari, Leelavathi sighed as a fleeting image appeared in her mind's eye of her younger self. She saw a strong woman with smooth ebony skin and bright, clear eyes set in a sharp but attractive face, with a mane of thick, jet-black hair down to her waist. Her current appearance, shriveled frame, wrinkled skin, bent fingers, and thin grey hair, held barely a glimpse of her past glory. Yet despite the ravages of time, such an occasion called for her best. And she was prepared to give it, despite her withered arthritic hands and far-from-glamorous appearance.

As eager as Leelavathi was to perform her opus, she was still a bit surprised to be here at the palace. After all, it did seem like a bit of a dream, the way she had come to this point. As she began to teach Rishab and, over time, word had spread of her teaching among friends and family. Then, one day a request arrived in the mail that changed everything for her. A successor of the Maharaja, the man who had saved her life, had issued a personal invitation for her to perform at the very palace she grew up in.

She brought her mind back to the present. One final concert. She had dreamed of this day for such a long time—from her girlhood, really. She had waited patiently for this moment and then, when her hands grew arthritic, had to deal with the disappointment of thinking this moment would never come.

Now she had the chance to heal the hurts and disappointments of the past and fill her soul with the sweet reverberations of her distant youth. For so long, she had shelved her urge to lay her hands on the strings that filled her with life and joy, but tonight she played with determination, inspiration, and joy—a winning combination, no matter the age of the musician.

About to play the veena on the palace stage, where her great-grandson

Rishab would accompany her by playing the tanpura, Leelavathi smiled to herself. She was pleased by this indication that he wanted to be a dedicated student and would carry on the family tradition. One of her greatest regrets was that she had not been able to pass on her love—and her father's love—of music to her son. Tonight, she had a second chance.

Leelavathi took another deep breath, steadying herself. How she wished her father could be here on this night. Despite that impossibility, she was dedicating this performance to him. Her secret wish had long been to fulfill his wish, initially for a son but then for his daughter, to be among the greatest musicians that India had ever seen.

This night, her final performance was more than just a concert put on by an ailing old musician. This represented the culmination of her musical career and a manifested dream. Since the court was disbanded during the British raj, now the place had been turned into a concert hall. She had never been given her chance to play at the palace and had thought it impossible. Yet here she was.

The years had been long and full. After being freed by the Maharaja, she and her son were reunited at last. She did not have to choose between music and her family; she had been fortunate to have a successful musical career, traveling with the troupe for many more years before settling down with her bandmate, Vishnu. Unfortunately, the constant movement of such a nomadic life had resulted in a more strained relationship with her son than she would have wished, and she was still trying to make amends for that. Leelavathi had played her veena daily until her old age caught up to the point that it could not be ignored, until Rishab discovered the instrument despite her best attempt to hide it away forever.

Still, her main regret remained that she had been unable to pass on her legacy to anyone. She had indeed failed to pass her talent on to her son and grandson, but tonight was her chance to carry on the family tradition through her great-grandson, Rishab. She would share what was left of her music, and of her, with this crowd and with him, a bright flash of light on the horizon that lingered long after the sun had set.

As she tried to recall the high points, Leela kept coming back to her father's dream. She had known from a young age that her career and musical talent was written in the stars on that auspicious day. An artist and musician at heart, nothing could deter her from practicing her art and passing on the oral traditions her father passed to her. As the daughter of a veena player, she thought she could play her father's instrument and could keep it alive and continue his work, though he was gone. This was her chance to give the veena, in the wooden box for so long, new life.

How had she locked her music in a box for so long? She shook her head at herself, still mystified at her own ability to lock the box so many years ago, believing it to be for the last time, vowing never to unlock it again. It was fitting, actually, that her resolve would be weakened by her love of a child. The talented Rishab, whose ardent pleas and curiosity persuaded her to reopen the case that held her magnificent veena and, in turn, unleashed her music and gave her hope again.

She looked down at the veena, with its large, flat, wooden resonator from which emerged a tapered neck that curved downward into the face of a dragon that, in turn, stared at the smaller, golden resonator below. She loved all of it from the metal frets fixed atop the neck, to the strings spanning its entire length, to the delicate ivory carvings lining its elegant edge.

The power of the veena, and the music she created on it was undeniable. Once the box was open, Leelavathi had begun to remember the days when the veena was the purpose of her life and how it sustained her through good times and bad. Yes, she had hidden it away until recent years, but no longer would her music be under lock and key. She would battle the pain of arthritis in her quest to unleash the instrument and music she loved until she had no more strength.

Leela gathered her thoughts, took one more deep breath, and stepped onto the stage with a broad smile. As she approached the straw mat where she would sit to give her concert, the applause began. Unlike the first public ovation of her life, which she didn't have a chance to savor, she would soak in the thunderous applause tonight. And, unlike the prison she found herself in before the Maharaja freed her, she would enjoy the satisfaction of knowing that she would not be forgotten. She would pass on her art, her joy, her love of the veena and its music to Rishab, who would do the same in good time, and she would become as unforgettable as her veena, a conduit of lovely melodies and beautiful music with the power to unleash the soul.